and all the t
Besides, in
pretend. "Tha

"The haircut is lovely, too." Maisie stood and poured Cate a cup of tea from a blue Spode pot. It smelled of caramel and vanilla. "I love that touch of silver coming through."

"Same cut as last time." Cate took the cup, her cheeks growing warm from the compliments.

Ellie flopped on a stool beside Maisie and groaned. "I can't make any more decisions and we still have to order more towels."

"At least the bed linens came in the mail this morning." Maisie closed the catalog and patted her friend's arm. "You're taking things too much to heart, Ells. I got this. Trust me." She turned to Cate. "Tell her to trust me."

"Trust Maisie, Ells." Cate sipped the fragrant tea. "I mean, truly. Look how beautiful Beach House is. The entire place is so elegant."

"Oh, elegant, I don't know," Ellie muttered pettily. "I'm more bohemian."

Maisie patted Ellie's arm one last time. "There there," she said consolingly. "How about we'll get one of those colorful cotton rugs for the laundry room."

Cate smiled and went to the fridge, spotting a bowl of freshly whipped cream. Allen would've taken it and flushed it down the toilet. But he wasn't here, and she spooned a good dollop into her tea.

"I'm not talking about the laundry room!" Ellie protested. "And I just don't know with the matchy curtains."

"White. Believe me." Maisie put a definite hand on her catalog.

"And you can have a yellow picture," Cate explained. "Maybe the Van Gogh sunflowers?"

Ellie threw her a withering look.

Cate grinned. "Or not. There'll be other pictures. TJ Maxx sometimes has good ones."

Maisie shook her head. "Excuse me; we're not hanging TJ Maxx on the walls of this house."

Cate had plenty of TJ on her own walls. It certainly looked nice enough, but Maisie was used to better. Her aristocratic husband had had a fine-art habit. The contents of several European castles were stored in the attic. "Are there any paintings upstairs that would work?" Cate asked.

"*Yellow*? Hmm." Maisie took off her glasses. "I'd have to go check."

Cate glanced at Ellie, who grinned back and topped up everyone's tea, pushing the cream to Cate.

Beach House had been built by a retired sea captain. He'd owned shipyards and harpoon factories at a time when fleets changed the fate of nations and sailors turned whales into enemies. Swimming in money like a minnow, the captain had spared no expense on his mansion.

Cate thought Beach House had about fifteen bedrooms. As if that wasn't enough space for a single family, the basement dug into the rock below practically connected to the Roman catacombs. The attic above was a never-ending story. It was quite possible that swamps and unicorns lurked in some unexplored corner.

They'd all known about Robert storing 'his things' in the attic. But Maisie had never bothered to look. First, because she'd had a son, and later, because she'd lost him.

Only when the inn had needed furniture had they all climbed the rickety staircase behind the butler's pantry.

They'd found plenty for their guestrooms—bed frames and armoires and desks of mahogany and rosewood and silver. There were gilded Venetian mirrors and rolled oriental rugs, stacks of oils in massive frames and tapestries woven in decades of busywork. They'd stumbled over boxes of crystal and cases of china, jade figurines and bronze sculptures and an iron armor lying on the ground like an empty nut, surly candelabras and glittering chandeliers. Doilies galore. Lace everywhere.

The attic truly harbored a treasure. It was breathtaking. Not least because it was so dusty that Sam hadn't been able to stop sneezing and Cate had had an asthma attack and they'd had to go find her inhaler.

At first, they'd called out over every treasure, delighted and eager to share with the others. By the end of the second day, they'd been exhausted and overwhelmed.

So much *stuff*.

Surveying her despondent crowd like a grimy queen, Maisie had put her hands on her hips, declared that a proper appraiser needed to do a proper job and that she'd take care of it when she'd get round to it, which would be soon.

She'd shooed everyone back down the rickety staircase and hired a few able-bodied men from the village to bring down what was needed. Then she'd left Sam and Cate overseeing the job while eating sponge cake on the patio, while she'd gone shopping with Ellie.

They'd returned from their trip to Bay Port with the trunk and backseat of Maisie's Acura filled with modern lamps and potted trees jutting between the seats, vines to soften corners and a load of milky-green vases for the yellow roses that grew in the garden.

Now, Ellie cleared her throat delicately. "How about it, Maise? Do you remember seeing a good picture upstairs, or should we buy one?"

Maisie eyed the ceiling of the kitchen as if the attic treasure might come crashing through. "There's got to be something in between a print from TJ's and the oils in the attic."

Cate smiled. Maisie had no intention of taking care of the things in the attic. Maybe if she ever needed money, she'd sell some pieces. Otherwise, she was clearly content leaving Robert's past to rest in peace.

"Tommy had that artwork from that guy," Ellie said helpfully. Tom, Ellie's son, ran the Beach Cove Corner Café, a small restaurant where local artists liked to hang their pieces. Nothing sold a painting like creamy tiramisu.

"That's right!" Cate knew at once what Ellie meant. "Those pictures were pretty."

"Why don't you ask Tom to recommend something?" Maisie stood to rinse her cup. "It'd be good to support someone from the community. It's got to be tasteful, though."

"Of course it'd be tasteful," Ellie said. "Tom knows what he's doing. Now let's give Cate a tour."

Cate had had many tours already, but she didn't mind one more. It was fun seeing the progress and imagining what she'd have done herself.

"Follow me." Maisie waved Cate out of the kitchen, and using a corridor splitting off to the left, they trotted to the old nursery wing. There were five bedrooms with a sitting room each, all with a fireplace and a view of the sea.

"Pretty as can be," Cate said after pacing the last room. "I was against felling the old sycamores in front of the windows, but I can't argue with how much brighter it is in here."

"Not to mention you can see the cove." Maisie pointed, and Cate stepped closer.

A few weeks ago, massive tree trunks and sweeping branches had hidden the field of goldenrod and sedum, pink and fluffy as morning clouds, that rolled toward the sea like a sweet-smelling carpet.

"I think you should start booking guests. This inn is ready," Cate said. "It doesn't get any better." Wistfully, she touched the pretty vase that stood, still empty, on the windowsill.

Both her friends had suffered. They deserved this

wealth and beauty.

Cate turned before she could think about herself. "Let's go back."

Maybe one day, her daughters would get married and there'd be weddings. That was something to look forward to. If she was lucky, there might even be grandchildren. Though Em was in no hurry to settle down. Sometimes, it worried Cate.

"Cate?" Maisie asked after they'd returned to the kitchen.

"Yes?"

"What do you think about staying with us for a while? It'd be fun." Maisie opened the fridge and pulled out a platter of serving-size strawberry shortcakes. "We need someone around test all the recipes we're trying out. Ellie always seems to have the opposite opinion to my own, and we want our guests to be happy with our food."

Maisie lowered two plump cakes on a plate, one from each side of the platter, and pushed it toward Cate. Glazed berries toppled like sweet promises from the cream. "For example, could you please try these two and tell me which one tastes better?"

"Yeah," Ellie said, narrowing her eyes. "Try the one on the right first. Here. This one." She turned the plate and pointed. Maisie shook her head, but she was smiling.

"Okay." Cate took the fork Maisie handed her and scooped a bite into her mouth. "Oh my goodness. Girls." She had another bite, closing her eyes to savor it. "This is *so* good."

"You can have the Jack and Jill both." Maisie sounded satisfied.

"Great." The Jack and Jill bedrooms were above the kitchen, next to Ellie's and opposite Maisie's room.

Cate tried the other cake. It was delicious, but she couldn't taste a difference from the first. "Hmm." She tried the first one again.

"I have to get started on the lava cake if I want to frost it before dinner." Ellie checked the clock on the wall. "I want you to have a slice for dessert. I think the chocolate we ordered has too much cocoa in it, but Maisie said it's supposed to be like that."

"I'll go get you fresh towels, Cate." Maisie hurried out of the kitchen. "And then I'll make *my* cake," they heard her call from the staircase. "Hope you like Viennese Sacher torte, Cate."

"We'll have coconut shrimp for dinner." Ellie pulled a cookbook from a shelf and flipped through it. "I read about them in a novel and wanted to try to make them ever since."

"I don't mind," Cate said and pointed at the cakes. "Quick—which one is yours and which one is Maisie's?"

Ellie grinned. "They're both Maisie's. It's a test."

"You two are getting worse by the day." Cate took a last bite. She was still stuffed from her lavish breakfast. "Well, tell her if anyone needs another reason to book a room, this cake is it."

"You're not full, are you?" Ellie glanced critically at the leftovers. "I need you to try Tom's macaroons really quick. He's got a new recipe that takes only half

19

the time, but he made a mistake telling the customers about it. Mrs. Odell stormed into the kitchen as soon as she heard it, demanding he bring the old recipe back. She'd never even tried the new recipe." She chuckled. "Poor kid, he can't keep up. He really needs a proper baker at the Café."

"I'm a bit of an expert on macaroons. Em's been perfecting her recipe for twenty years. She made her first when she was six and hasn't stopped." Cate pulled out a stool and sat. She'd been looking forward to her alone-time at home, but maybe she'd been wrong. Maybe what she truly needed was strawberry shortcake and coconut shrimps. And friends.

Chapter 3

All through the year, even when the sand burned swimmers' feet and made them hop and skip to the water, Beach Cove mornings were misty mornings.

True Beach Covians who grew up under the sea's spell loved the calm of fog, the break it offered from day and duty. Newcomers on the other hand struggled with anything from damp socks to wandering far into tidal flats. But they never actually died when the flats flooded, and after a year or so of fruitless resistance, most of them resigned themselves to embracing the magic.

Of course it wasn't magic but the cove's warm water. Shielded by cliffs, only a trickle of the cold Atlantic current that fed the bay also reached the cove.

This morning, the fog was as soft and slow as a lazy tabby.

Quietly, Cate stepped outside, shutting the front door behind her. Ellie and Maisie were still asleep. The night before, they'd sat until late on the patio, sipping jasmine tea and watching the moon cross the cove. Cate would've liked to stay up longer with them, but by ten o'clock, her eyes burned. Years of teaching had trained Cate to the rhythm of school days.

On the plus side, now she could enjoy a morning walk on the beach and still be back to brew coffee and scramble eggs before her friends woke.

Cate pulled her knit jacket tight as she walked down the driveway, grateful for her long skirt that reached down to her rubber boots. The fog would be even thicker down at the beach, and clammy.

She followed a path along the side of the house to the spot where the old sycamores had stood. When she got there she paused, wondering about the years of shelter the trees had given. They'd worked hard to protect Beach House from wind and shade it from heat, and yet the space was so much more cheerful now they were gone. It was hard to miss them even though the trees had been special this far north, only growing because of the warm cove. But they belonged to the rich captain and his harpoons, not the inn with ocean view apartments.

Cate put her hand on the rough plate of a stump and traced an age line. There was one for each year that had passed, but many were hidden under resin and splinters. Slivers of wood that had built something as solid as a sycamore.

Cate wondered whether the years had been like the hidden lines, forgotten themselves but building the present. Some human lives were like that. Most lives, maybe.

Hers, certainly.

She broke off a small splinter to carry and then followed the dewy field down to the beach.

The sand was wet from the tide. Cate's boots left deep impressions, but the waves filled them with white froth, smoothing the sand before retreating again. Cate stopped and looked back. The water washed away any trace of her steps. Was it a good thing not to leave a trace? Cate didn't know.

The next time she stopped, Cate dropped the sycamore splinter into the water. She didn't want it. She didn't want her life to be like that.

A sound made her look up. It didn't come from the invisible sandpipers peeping at the waves or the gulls flapping through the fog like shrunken pterodactyls.

It sounded like feet sloshing in water. Someone was walking towards her.

Cate's heart stumbled into her throat, and she gulped air to shove it back down. "Silly," she murmured. Because hearing the steps, she'd automatically thought of Calvin.

Calvin, who ran the pharmacy and who was smart and funny.

Calvin, who had liked Cate for a few weeks in the summer.

They'd gone on a date. It'd been during the middle of the day in full view of the public, and they'd only eaten ice cream and walked to the harbor. But they'd walked arm in arm, and they'd laughed too much.

And then Cate had changed her mind.

She was married. She had children who needed her.

But every time she walked into the village, her eyes were drawn to the pharmacy. Every time she turned around, she scanned for Calvin's face. And every time she heard a noise, she apparently expected him.

Unfortunately, life wasn't a cheesy movie. Calvin wouldn't appear, take her hands, gaze into her soul and urge her to elope with him.

Cate squinted, trying to see who else was trapped with her in the fog. The splashing became louder and the fog started to swirl, revealing a silhouette.

Slim, tall, unfamiliar.

The woman materialized like a ghost. When she spotted Cate, she stopped short and stared.

Cate stared back.

Because she knew the person after all. Knew her very well, even though she'd never thought to see her here.

Cate clasped her hands to keep them from shaking. "Helene?"

Her sister opened her mouth as if she wanted to say something, maybe yes, or maybe hello, or Cate's name. But nothing came out, and she closed it again. The fine green-blue eyes narrowed, and with a movement Cate remembered well, Helene swiped a strand of platinum hair back. Then she shoved her hands into the pockets of a waxed jacket.

Cate waited. It'd been years since they'd met. Twenty-seven years. Cate had been very pregnant with Em back then. She'd only just made Maisie's acquaintance. The old woman on the cliff had been dead for only a week.

How did Helene come to walk on this beach?

Didn't she know Cate lived in Beach Cove?

A wave licked the rolled-up cuffs of Helene's jeans, and she stepped higher onto the sand. "I've been looking for you, Cate."

Cate's mouth felt dry and salty. Helene's voice was as high and clear as she remembered. It was a beautiful voice. Mother had always said it was a rare soprano and the most beautiful voice in the United States. One time, she'd even said the world.

Cate had never forgotten about the rare soprano, though she'd never known what exactly the rare element was. She only knew it was rare. Reserved for the best.

"You came for me?" The fog muffled Cate's own, perfectly ordinary voice. She cleared her throat. "You want to see me, Helene?"

"Yes, Cate," Helene said. "Why else would I be here?"

The water sucked the sand out from under Cate's heels, making her sink. "Why?" she asked. "It's been so long. Why do you want to see me now?"

Helene tossed her hair back. "Not because I miss you," she replied. "I need to sort out a few things. Strictly for my own mental health."

"Okay," Cate said after a pause. What was wrong with Helene's mental health? She'd always been strong.

But childhood hadn't been a comfortable ride. Not for her, not for Helene. Maybe it'd been Mother's grip, not Helene herself, that'd been strong.

"How about a cup of tea?" Cate asked.

Her sister frowned as if the offer annoyed her. But then she nodded. "Where?"

Cate turned and pointed back at the inn. The haze was now thinning enough to reveal the stately mansion.

Like a stronghold, Cate thought. Beach House was a safe place. If she brought Helene there, nothing could happen because Cate's friends lived in the house. They'd have her back. No matter what Helene would say or do.

"This way." Cate turned without waiting, sure Helene wouldn't want to walk beside her. She sensed her sister's impatience like pinpricks between her shoulder blades. Helene always walked ahead of Cate. Reversing the order felt awkward, like holding a kid's hand the wrong way.

Cate was older. But Helene was *better*.

Because Helene had been Mother's shining star.

Cate had not been a star. Cate had been a disappointment, failing Mother all the way into the grave.

They'd reached the stairs, and Cate started to climb. Lifting her long, heavy skirt, she felt like a servant from the olden days. Walking behind her was the young lady, her sister.

Beautiful, rich and very angry.

Chapter 4

"So this is it?" Sam asked. The street seemed to disappear in the morning haze as she focused on her husband. The long nose, the thin, masculine lips, the intelligent eyes. She'd not see them again anytime soon because Larry was leaving.

Only for a year, only for a research trip.

Sam knew she shouldn't mind so much; she wasn't sentimental. But it felt like Larry was leaving *her*. Like he was leaving forever. She pressed her hands to her stomach and ordered herself not to whine.

Because Larry wanted this. He wanted this, even though she didn't, and all the wheels were moving, and nothing could be stopped.

"Just for a while," Larry murmured. Regret swung in his voice, and that surprised her. "Just for six months, Sam. Then I'll come visit and we'll see each other. At least for a week. Maybe two." He put a finger under her chin and lifted it.

The grad student behind the car's steering wheel averted his eyes, Sam was about to purse her lips, and then Larry dropped her chin and lifted his carryall instead.

She blinked and stepped back, letting fog swirl around her. "Goodbye, Larry. Take care of yourself."

He squeezed her elbow. "You too, Samantha."

Using her full name made it sound like a warning, and his touch wasn't tender. Sam pulled away and rubbed the spot where he'd gripped her. "I'll be fine," she said. "You're the one traveling around the globe."

"Promise me you'll be safe, Sam. No nonsense."

What nonsense? She was going to sit in her bookstore all day, every day. It hardly compared to hunting down illegally smuggled Syrian manuscripts in rural Turkey. Sam shrugged. It was too late to argue. "I promise. No swimming on a full belly."

Larry looked like he wanted to say something more. But he only hitched his carryall higher, pecked her cheek and strode around the car's hood. The grad student hastily leaned across the passenger seat to open the door, and Larry folded himself inside the sedan.

Sam followed him, bending at the waist for a last glimpse through the window. The driver nodded at her, obviously satisfied the emotional phase of the pickup was over. He revved the engine hopefully.

Larry looked back at Sam. He smiled, but she knew he was worried. The groove between his eyes was a dead giveaway.

Sam motioned for him to roll down the window.

Of course he was worried. In his mind, a lot was at stake. The trip was the cumulation of four years of research and scheming and writing grant proposals to study an armful of old manuscripts.

Sam had never understood why his contact refused to send photographs. Sometimes, the man wanted to see cash first. The photos didn't turn out, or he didn't have a camera. The explanations changed, according to Larry.

Now, he ignored Sam's gesture to roll down the window. Instead he waved and turned to his student, who grinned like a sheep and reached for the gearshift.

Sam straightened. She'd known it'd be like this. No kisses or last words. That's how it was for them.

The car drove off gingerly, the student tipsy or overly intimated by Larry's presence.

It didn't matter that he'd not kissed her properly. She was forty-five, after all. Standing on her own two feet. She hadn't kissed *him* either.

Sam glanced at the sky. An hour ago, it'd been as thick as clam chowder, but now the sun burned patches of blue into the cover. Another hour and the patches would merge into an azure dome.

Maybe she'd skip work and go to the beach while it was still warm enough.

It wasn't so bad, living here. Even on her own.

Maybe it'd be fun... Larry was a complex person. It'd be lonely living without him. Quite possibly, it'd be easier, too.

The asters waved from behind the crooked fence of Sam's crooked Victorian, eagerly outlining the path to the front door for her. The toasty fragrance of batch-roasted coffee suddenly beckoned from the kitchen window.

Clearly, Sam was supposed to come inside. She knew there'd be a book waiting on her spot on the couch. Sam also knew she'd never find out who put it there. Maybe Larry. Maybe her own forgetful self. Maybe the house.

The book would be good. The coffee, too.

Cheered, Sam ambled through the front yard, trailing a hand over dripping bee balm and sodden fern fronds. After she stepped inside, the front door closed with a satisfied thud, as if the house was saying that having Larry around was nice, sure, but they certainly didn't need him.

In the living room, Sam glanced at the couch. A novel she didn't know; one of the books she'd inherited from her great-grandaunt Mimi.

She left it where it was and went into the kitchen. She still had an hour before it was time to open her bookstore.

Freedom, she thought suddenly.

For a *year*. Alone, at liberty to do exactly as she liked. Nobody to comment on her cooking, nobody to change the channel or leave socks on the bathroom floor, nobody who'd—

Her phone buzzed. Sam pulled it from her pocket, looked at the screen and swiped.

"Is he gone?" Ellie asked, sounding eager.

"Just now." Sam glanced at the clock on the windowsill. "Not even a minute yet."

"Oh good," Ellie said. "Why don't you come over? No need to be gloomy."

"Um." Sam cast around for an excuse. "I can't. I

have to get to the store."

"Don't lie, Samantha. You still have an hour. The wish to isolate yourself is a depression settling in. If you don't come here, we'll come to you."

Somewhere in the background, Maisie laughed. "I told you not to call her."

"I'm not depressed. I'm grateful to have a moment to myself, and that's different." Sam sighed, knowing it was useless. "I'm not going to waste my breath arguing. I'll be there in ten."

"Because we have cake. And we want to hear how it went," Ellie explained.

Sam knew she meant Larry's departure. They'd want to know if he'd kissed her. Sometimes, her friends behaved like fifteen-year-old girls, not fifty-year-old women.

Maisie called, "Tell her I'm making fresh coffee!"

"Coffee, got it," Sam said resignedly. She'd read the book later. After work, in the tub.

"We can have lunch and dinner together, too." Ellie lowered her voice to a whisper. "Did he give you a proper kiss goodbye?"

Sam coughed delicately. "His student was watching. It wasn't practical."

"Aha," Ellie said, suddenly brisk again. "Cate's gone on a morning walk, but she'll be back soon. We'll see you shortly."

Sam ended the call feeling as if she had an appointment with a meddlesome therapist.

But at least there'd be cake.

Chapter 5

By the time Cate reached the patio, the rising sun was drying the air. The breeze carried the salty, sandy fragrance of stranded rockweed.

She slowed, unsure what to do next. Ask Helene inside? Ellie and Maisie might be up, possibly still in PJ's and under-caffeinated. But it also felt wrong to ask her sister to wait outside like a stranger while Cate made tea in the kitchen.

"This is your house?" Helene looked around the estate, her gaze traveling from conservatory to guest wing, the garden, the way the goldenrod sloped toward the sea.

"Oh, no." It hadn't occurred to Cate Helene might think that. "I live closer to town. This is my friend's place."

"Your friend?" Helene made it sound as if Cate couldn't have friends.

"Wait here." Cate kicked off her rubber boots and slipped into the Birkenstocks she'd left by the patio door. "I'll go make the tea and bring it out."

Helene picked a chair and sat, pointing to the other. "I don't need tea, Cate. Sit."

Of course Helene didn't need tea. Cate didn't need tea either, but sometimes the pretense of civility was helpful.

Cate sat. "How are you, Helene?" she asked after a long silence.

"I'm fine," Helene said curtly. Then she rolled her shoulders as if she were in a boxing ring. "I'm doing fine," she relented. "I'm running a talent agency in LA. Managing models, actors, singers. A-list clientele, some B. It's financially rewarding. And I'm engaged." She lifted her hand to flash a diamond the size of a grape.

"Congratulations. I'm glad for you," Cate said, wondering whether it was a first marriage. Helene was in her forties. "It sounds like you found the perfect career, too." People loved Helene; she excelled as much at networking as at singing.

Cate glanced at her sister. After getting voted out of American Voice in the before-last round, Mother had vowed Helene would show everyone yet. She'd be richer than all the judges put together.

Brand-new Barbour jacket, Hermès silk scarf, platinum hair and fruit-sized diamond. It looked as if Helene had delivered.

Cate leaned forward. "Why exactly are you here, Helene? Is it about Mother?" The question was unnecessary. If it was about mental health, it was about Mother. And yet, they had to start somewhere.

Twenty-seven years ago last Thursday, Mother had died from complications of kidney disease. Twenty-seven years later, Helene's anger was still palpable. Like tar cloying the air, it numbed the taste buds in Cate's mouth, dried her tongue and clogged her nose. She rubbed it.

"It's about everything," Helene said. Again she rolled her shoulders like a boxer trying to relax between rounds. "And about the last day of Mother's life."

Cate's back itched as memories crawled up her spine. "I told you, Helene. Mother didn't want me in the hospital. She told me to get out. I know she told *you* I stormed out, hopping mad I couldn't get my hands on your share of the inheritance. But that's not what happened. I didn't storm out, and I never thought about money for a moment."

She waited until Helene looked up. "Helene, Mother lied. She lied all the time. I don't think she could help it."

"She did not." Each word was a chip of ice. "*You* do."

They'd come this far before. In the past, this was when arguments knitted into a loop and Cate gave up.

But she wasn't young and alone anymore. She was older and had daughters. She had friends, real friends here in Beach Cove, who loved her.

"I'm not lying, Helene," Cate repeated. "Can you listen to me? Mother told me she couldn't stand me. She said I had to leave, or she'd call security." Cate cleared her throat. "What could I do? I'm her daughter, too; I *wanted* to be with her. I'd hoped..." Her gaze dropped to her hands. They were big and ugly, and she pushed them into her sleeves. "I'd hoped Mother would say she loved me after all. Or at least let me tell her how much I loved her. But..."

The finger, hovering over the call button. The glare in Mother's eyes, the knowledge Cate would never look into them again, would never get another chance.

As always, the memory came with tears. Cate bit her lip so they wouldn't spill. "There was nothing I could do," she said flatly.

Helene frowned. "You yelled about your inheritance and stormed off. She told me as soon as I arrived. It took so much out of her. She was crying. Heartbroken. I can't forgive myself for not getting to the hospital sooner."

Cate pinched the skin between her thumb and finger, using the pinpoint of pain to focus. The doctors had assured her over and over that the kidney disease had caused the second stroke, not Cate's visit. "I think her heart broke long before she had children," she said quietly. Mother hadn't talked about her childhood. But sometimes hints had escaped her, bits and pieces of a past as cold and hard as lumps of coal.

Helene slumped back in her chair. "Why am I doing this?"

"Good question." Cate hadn't asked for the visit; she didn't want to relive the trauma. "Why are you here? Why travel across the country when you won't consider what I say?"

Helene opened her eyes. "Because apparently, I have to."

"You *have* to?"

"I need to heal my relationships, so I can become as whole and successful as I deserve to be."

"I see." She sounded like one of Cate's students after getting a hold of auntie's self-help book. Cate pinched her hand again, using her fingernails, letting welts rise on the skin.

Something else rose as well. Anger at still being made the family scapegoat. The one to blame. The one whose fault it all was.

Cate swallowed, choking the fury back down as hard as the tears earlier. Harder, even.

Tears were weak, but anger was an alien. It was a stranger in her chest, throttling Cate from the inside. It was dangerous. It could be fatal.

Mother had been an angry woman. Her wrath had bubbled inside a volcano of smiles and bottle-blond hair, erupting only in the secrecy of the family room or kitchen.

Nobody saw. Nobody knew, and nobody helped.

Cate inhaled the briny air, letting go when she exhaled.

She'd been six when she'd learned how to let go of anger. A cup had broken; the good one with the white bird on it. Cate had been playing hopscotch when Mother called her inside, pointed at the shards, and then slapped Cate's face so hard her braids went flying. Cate's vision blurred with shock and fear and anger, making everything vibrate. She hadn't been in the house, and she never touched the forbidden cup. And so, without thinking, Cate hit Mother back. Hard, her fingers rolled into a fist. It left a pink spot on Mother's leg.

Because of her anger, Cate didn't get any food for three days after the cup broke. The hunger scratched her belly and made her weak until she didn't want to walk anymore and couldn't remember her letters in school. She didn't know when Mother would let her eat again. She thought it was possible she would die.

And so she had learned.

Her anger was a raindrop, while Mother's was an ocean. The raindrop never won; it was always swallowed whole. Faced with an ocean, it couldn't exist.

Now, Helene stirred in her patio chair. "You're still making that puffing sound," she said. Her veiled eyes didn't show whether it was an accusation or concern for her sister's health.

"I'm not going to lie to make you more whole, Helene," Cate replied. "I don't think I can help you."

"I should've known you don't care." Helene's back didn't touch the chair. "At least admit you tried to cut me out of the inheritance. You and your husband."

Cate frowned. "Allen has nothing to do with this."

"He hates me. And you always take his side. Over your own—" Her chest caved, and she gasped, looking almost surprised. "Over your own *sister*."

Cate raised her hands in frustration. "That last day? I was crying on the phone, and he told me to come home. Any husband would. Where else was I supposed to go after Mother threw me out?"

"He's had you under his thumb from the very beginning. Until you admit that he was more important to you than your mother—or Dad, or—" Helene pressed a hand to her collarbone. "*All* of us, I can't… We can't…"

Cate exhaled slowly, as if it could help Helene do the same. "Can't what? Be a family again? You and me and Dad?" Dad had always lived quietly in the background, making money, looking the other way. Cate knew it was easier for him if she wasn't in his life.

Helene's features narrowed into a mask. "Cate, Dad died. Four years ago."

The news dizzied Cate. She'd known this would happen. She'd known they wouldn't tell her.

But *four* years?

"You could've called me." Cate blinked. "You could've let me know. It would've made a difference, Helene."

"You never called. You didn't *care*." Helene almost yelled the last word. It hung like a sharp cloud over the lavender.

Cate shrugged; she couldn't speak. There was nothing to say. Helene had been the golden child for a reason; she was everything Mother had wanted to be. Beautiful, a natural socialite, a gifted singer. Because she'd been so adored, Helene didn't know and couldn't see. She'd never been on the outside, looking in.

"Cate, I don't understand. Why don't you care? Why did you leave me?"

Cate looked up. "I care for the same reason I can't leave you. We're sisters." The waves rushed louder, as if the sea wanted to comment.

"Mother said you envied me. You hated me."

All the nights they'd slept in the same bed because Mother was being scary, all the tricks they'd shared to make it through the days. Had Helene forgotten how it'd been when they were little? Before Mother had noticed they were stronger together?

"I adored you," Cate said. "Don't you remember? You were all I had."

Helene shook her head.

"I know who you are, Helene. I know you in a way no one else can." Cate stood. She was cold and exhausted and wanted her friends. "I only fell out of touch because I had no choice."

Chapter 6

"There you are! We were starting to wonder where you'd gotten to." Ellie held the patio door for Maisie, who was carrying their filled-to-the-rim cups, then followed slowly. The vibe was off.

Cate looked like a spooked horse, and a stranger sulked on one of the chairs. Expensive lawyer-type, too posh to be local. Where'd she come from? And why was she bugging Cate?

Maisie set the cups on the table and shook the heat from her fingertips. "Who's your friend, Cate?" she asked. And then, more cautiously, "Would you like coffee?"

Ellie frowned. She'd never seen the woman before. A little younger, icy eyes, perfectly put together. Lots of money for sure. "Who are you?" Ellie demanded.

Cate blinked. "This is Helene."

"Who?"

"Your *sister* Helene?" Maisie asked.

"Yes." Helene stood. "I'm not going to bother you. I was leaving."

"Cate? Ellie and I can just—" Maisie gestured at the house.

"Where are you staying, Helene?" Cate asked.

"A place in... Sandpiper Inn? I've got it in my GPS." Helene pursed her mouth, as if the Sandpiper Inn's address didn't deserve memorizing.

It was a nice inn, though. Golf course and everything. Dale had written letters to Bonnie there.

Ellie crossed her arms. Cate had told them about Helene years ago, and Ellie hadn't liked what she'd heard.

Helene-The-Golden, favorite child of Mother Catherine whose biggest regret in life had been accidentally bestowing her name on the wrong daughter.

Mommy Dearest, Ellie had thought when she'd heard the stories.

"Are you going to come back so we can talk more?" Cate asked.

"Do you want me to?" Helene's gaze slid down to Cate's feet and back.

"Yes. Do you?"

The younger woman hesitated but then held out a hand.

Cate clasped it for a moment. Helene pulled away and left, taking the patio steps two at a time. She strode toward the beach without looking back.

Ellie went to Cate and put an arm around her.

"Way to exit." Even Maisie sounded annoyed. "*Very* dramatic." She tasted her coffee, then poured both cups into the potted azalea. "Cold."

Ellie huffed. Helene could stay away because Cate had enough to deal with at home. They'd talked about it after Cate went to bed. She tried harder than any of them to make her marriage work against all odds. Soon, they were afraid, something had to give.

"Cate? Are you coming inside?" Ellie wanted to make Cate comfortable, give her honey toast and hot tea to pull her back. "Sam's on her way over. You can tell us what happened."

"She walked out of the fog just like that," Cate said. "I think she wants to be in touch again."

"Are you sure?" Maisie raised an eyebrow. "Be careful, Cate. Maybe Helene wants drama. Your mother only got in touch when she wanted to build you up for the kick of cutting you down later. Narcissism is generational, and Helene was your mother's pet. Whether or not she's aware, she likely picked up some abusive behaviors."

Ellie nodded, impressed. Maisie was poise herself, but she didn't mince words when she had an opinion.

"Maybe," Cate said. "But maybe not. She's my sister."

Ellie bit her tongue. Helene, Mother Dearest, Allen.

Hopeless relationships were Cate's curse.

But there was no sense in saying it because Cate already knew Ellie's opinion. Ellie had told her plenty of times. They all had. Unfortunately, the woman was more healer than warrior. She never got angry, and she never gave up on a person.

"Hot drink," Ellie declared and clapped her hands. "With cream. And breakfast. You haven't eaten anything, and I made scones that are to-die-for. Em's recipe, actually, we stole it. Come on, Cate. You're all cold." She dragged Cate into the sunroom where it was cozy and warm and sat her in a wicker chair. "Stay here."

Cate did, and Ellie continued into the kitchen. She was spooning cream on plates in the kitchen when the doorbell rang. Maisie went to open it and returned with Sam, who also wanted a plate with scones, lingonberry jam and cream.

Soon, they were all sitting in the sunroom, first or second breakfast on their knees, mugs steaming on the side tables. Cate told Sam about her encounter. For a while they ate in silence, waiting for the color to return to Cate's cheeks.

"Okay, so." Sam licked jam off a fingertip. "What exactly did Helene say, Cate?"

Cate told them what she remembered. After she'd finished, Sam brought her hands down on the arms of her chair with a soft pat. "I'm so sorry about your Dad, Cate. But don't let Helene upset you—there isn't much she can do to you, other than make your relationship better. We're here if you need backup." She picked up her empty cup. "I have to get to the store. Thanks for breakfast, Ells. It was good."

"Feeling better?" Maisie asked.

"I didn't feel bad in the first place." Sam stood. "I only came because you said I had to."

Ellie winked at her. It was fun messing with Sam. If they had a warrior in the bunch, it was her. But under the crusty outer layer bubbled *so* much—

Sam glowered at Ellie. "What?"

Ellie pursed her lips. "Don't think just because Larry's gone you can lock yourself away to cook up your witchy recipes. You'll get depressed." Sam's ancestors had been notorious for authoring recipes, and Sam took her moldy cookbooks way too seriously.

"I wasn't going to cook up anything," Sam said. "Because I already did. The recipes are no good."

"Not a single one?" Maisie smiled. "Do they need magic to work?"

"I'm sure," Sam said dryly.

"Can *I* try them out? Maybe I'll have more luck." Ellie wiggled her eyebrows.

Sam didn't even let them see the books. They were locked in a secret hideaway, though it was probably just the high shelf in Sam's pantry. The pantry key would be hidden under the microwave, or maybe the coffee maker. Sam was too straightforward.

Sam narrowed her eyes into slits. "I want two days of nobody calling me."

Maisie drummed her fingers on her knee. "You've got it, darling. We'll wait until you've had time to bore yourself."

Sam turned to leave through the garden but stopped when her gaze fell on the table. Ellie remembered Sam asking several times before about the next opportunity for a patio party. "Bye," Sam said again, sounding a little deflated.

"Maybe one day of no calling?" Ellie suggested. "Cate's going to show us how to make fruit tarts. We could eat them on the patio with homemade ice cream. Strawberry. What do you say, Sammy?"

Sam ran a hand through her straight, white-blond hair. It used to be cut in a short pixie, but now the tips brushed her shoulders. "Yeah," she said. "Okay. If it's strawberry, I'll come."

They watched her walk away, picking a sprig of lavender on her way to the gate.

"She's going to be okay without Larry," Cate said. "Right?"

"Of course," Maisie said. "A little bit lonely, maybe."

"I wished he'd not gone off the way he did," Ellie muttered. Dale had fallen for another woman. Even though she was glad to be rid of him, the betrayal still hurt.

"It's different, Ellie," Cate said as if she'd read her thoughts. "He begged Sam to come to Turkey with him. She just didn't want to go."

"He only asked after he'd already decided to leave," Ellie said. "He should've stayed in Beach Cove when she said no."

"I'm not so sure," Maisie said gently. "He's got to do his job."

"There are better ways of doing a job than arranging a year in Turkey and informing your wife over a fish sandwich." Ellie had just about had it with men. She frowned at Cate. "What's going on with Allen?"

Maisie raised an eyebrow. "Easy, tiger."

"Oh, he's still gone." As usual, Cate brushed the topic off. "He texted it might be a bit longer than usual. Two weeks maybe? He wasn't specific."

Ellie's ears pricked up as if brush crackled under a predator's paws. "He's not left-left, has he?"

"I doubt it." Cate sounded almost as wry as Sam. "Though he could've picked a better time to disappear on me. When I went to water the plants yesterday, there was a strange car parked outside."

"Why strange? The tourists park their cars all over town."

"Not in my street. I'm not so close to the village that you would walk," Cate said.

The locals referred to the historic center of Beach Cove as the village. It had sidewalks and quaint stores, a marketplace with a fountain and rhododendrons, benches to sit and eat a piece of saltwater taffy. There was also a small harbor for fishing vessels and an even smaller marina for sailboats.

"I suppose they could've been there for your beach," Ellie said. There was a small one close to Cate's, though it had its own parking lot. But the weather still drew a crowd now and then. Maybe it'd been full.

Cate shrugged. "If they came for a swim, why didn't they get out of the car?"

Maisie tilted her head. "They stayed in the car? What were they doing? Talking?"

"No." Cate shifted, and the wicker chair crackled. "They were looking at my house. For half an hour? Maybe an hour."

"Two men were watching your house for an hour?"

"The windows were tinted, but I saw their faces turned toward me. I even waved, though they didn't wave back. Just watched until I drove away."

"You waved?" Ellie asked weakly.

"There's not much else I can do," Cate said. "I can't call the police. It's a public street."

"Maybe building rapport is a good strategy." Maisie made it sound like a joke, like it was normal to have two men in a car with tinted windows sit and watch your place.

"That's what I figured." Cate nodded. "I think if they're there later today, I'll knock on their window and offer them fruit tarts. See how they respond."

"Apricot's the best," Maisie said. "They can't burn down your house if you offer them apricot tarts. We'll make them extra sweet."

"Maisie, don't encourage her." It wasn't funny.

Cate suddenly perked up. "Maybe they were waiting for Em to come home?"

Ellie shook her head to make sure she'd heard correctly. "Cate, I get you want Emily to find someone already. I feel the same way about Tom. But if some guy—*guys*—sit in a dark car in your street, that's not friendly. That's stalking. Statistically, stalkers are quite likely to turn into murderers. You don't want to feed that lot tarts. Let alone apricot."

Cate slumped back. "I better tell Em and Claire to watch out," she said. "I didn't know about the murder part."

Chapter 7

Em's phone buzzed. She fished it out of the back pocket of her jeans and glanced at the screen. Mom was leaving the inn to check at the house. Em silenced the phone and slipped it back.

"You don't have very much time to decide." Regina checked her own cell. Em knew Regina's three young sons and her job as Beach Cove's only real estate agent kept her busy. "It's hitting the market tomorrow if you don't take it today."

"I'll take it." Outside the living room window, an old oak waved its leaves. In the winter, when the foliage was gone, she'd have a view of Tom's Corner Café.

"And there's the two-month deposit?" Regina made it sound like a question, and Em's stomach tightened. She didn't have the deposit.

"Um—I'll let you know by tonight, is that okay?" Mom would loan her the deposit if she had it, but... Maybe Em could get credit at the bank.

Somehow, she had to scrape the money together. She couldn't stand Dad's silent anger any longer. Claire needed out, too. At the last family dinner, her little sister had sat so straight and quiet, so scared of annoying Dad with sounds of chewing or drinking or whatever it was he hated that night, it broke Em's heart.

The corner of Regina's mouth trembled with stress. Or was it pity? "Okay. That's fine. Only...I can't keep it off the market, Em. There are too many people looking for something like this."

"Yes, I know. I'll call either way." Em hitched the strap of her farmer's market tote higher, feeling a stab of annoyance. Not at Regina, who was doing Em a huge favor, but at herself.

If she'd had any guts, she could be well on her way to becoming a heart surgeon. She'd be doing residency now, earning more than enough for the apartment. Enough to protect Claire.

Instead, she'd chickened out. She couldn't stand seeing blood and vessels and pulsing life cracked open.

Now she was teaching acting classes at the community college and wondered how on earth she was going to scrape together a thousand dollars for a one-bedroom in one of Beach Cove's two old brownstones.

Regina checked her phone again. "Do you want to walk through one more time?"

Yes, Em wanted to. In fact, she never wanted to leave. But living with Dad had taught her to take careful notice of people's body language, and it wasn't hard to see Regina's barely suppressed panic.

"I love everything about it. I don't need to see it

again," Em said. "Actually, I have to go. Thanks for showing me the place, Regina. I'll cut off my toe to get the deposit." She turned and opened the door. The staircase smelled odd but not unpleasant. A bit like wet bread and disinfectant, with a whiff of the wisteria climbing the old brick outside.

Regina breathed an audible sigh of relief as she locked the apartment. Her phone beeped again when they were on the stairs and again when they left the building. "I have to run. I'm sorry. Ben's dizzy, and the coach just texted to come pick him up. Let me know." She pressed a card in Em's hand. A nod to professionalism even though they'd exchanged numbers years ago.

"Thanks again." Em watched Regina set off at a jog, waving over her shoulder.

Regina's boys were in Em's acting class. They couldn't behave for a minute straight, but under the grass-stains and bravado were sweet souls. It didn't hurt that they had angelic singing voices and loved acting as long as it required lots of running and jumping.

Regina was only ten years older than Em, but she lived in a different world entirely. Em didn't want to have kids. Never ever. She couldn't bear the responsibility.

Em sighed. That was a special talk with Mom she wasn't looking forward to. Mom had probably wanted grandkids since the age of ten. She wasn't dropping hints yet, but she sure was waiting with bated breath for Em to find a man and start talking babies. It was enough to give a girl a nightmare.

Em started walking. She had to make a thousand dollars in…what? Six, seven hours. For a non-surgeon, there wasn't an honest way to make that sort of money in that time.

When she next looked up, she'd reached the fountain. The sun was almost at its zenith, the fog was gone, and it was getting hot. Locals and tourists strolled across the marketplace, herding kids, pointing at the day lilies.

Over at the Corner Café, every single table looked occupied. The scent of roasted garlic bread, seafood pizza and waffle fries wafted over. Em's mouth watered, but she had to make money, not spend it. She sat on the sandstone rim of the fountain and dipped her hand into the water. It was cold and silvery and a little bit like being on vacation.

For a moment, Em saw the reflection of a face she'd not seen in a long while. Not in a decade, and never again. She knew that. She closed her eyes and when she looked up, there was nobody standing over her.

There was, however, someone striding toward her.

Em shook her hand dry. "Hi, Tom," she called, and a few of the Café patrons turned to catch a glimpse of the chef.

"Hi, Em."

She smiled. Tom was the closest she had to a brother. Once upon a time, they'd fought over the best pacifiers and rattles. Later, they'd pooled their pocket money to buy video games and chocolate bars. A little later still, they'd helped each other survive the loss of their best friend. "Busy much?" she asked.

Tom sat on the pool beside her and closed his eyes dramatically. "So busy. But hey. I'm not complaining." He opened one eye and grinned. "Beats going broke."

Spring had been hard on his Café. All small businesses had struggled because Alex's bones had finally been found and laid to rest. The story, distorted and scandalized by the media, had kept the tourists away.

Em rubbed her temple as if she could rub the memory away. "You're definitely not going broke." She nodded at the full tables. "Is it hard to keep up with all the orders for clam chowder and lemon meringue?"

"I've got enough people to cook, but nobody can bake. I don't know what it is. Mikey was willing to try, but his sponge cake came out flat as his foot and about as tasty. No hope whatsoever." Tom scanned the crowd, then glanced at Em. With an embarrassed shrug, he lifted his long, black apron and pulled a pack of cigarettes from his jeans pocket.

"Oh no, Tom. Tell me you haven't started smoking." Em stood. She'd seen lung tumors in med school. "I'm leaving if you light up. I already lost one friend for no reason at all."

"Ah." Tom frowned at the pack. It was open at the corner, and from the way the paper wrinkled, it was clear a few sticks were missing. "You know, I can't stand the taste anyway." He held out the cigarettes, offering them to her.

"Good man." Em took the pack, aimed and chucked it in the nearest bin. Then she sat back down and leaned on Tom, wrapping both hands around his arm. "That bad, huh?"

"Yeah." Tom let his head rest on hers; heavy but comforting. Like one of those blankets filled with beads kids use to feel safe at night. "That bad."

"How long have you smoked, Tom?" Em asked. "Since you found Alex?"

He straightened, taking the warm weight off her head. "Yep."

"Well, stop again. For me, if not your health. I'm still here. Yeah?"

"Okay."

She nodded, satisfied Tom would keep the promise.

"I better get back, Em."

"But you just got out." She tightened her grip. "Do you even take a lunch break?"

"Sure."

"Oh, please." Em let him go so she could look at him. "First you smoke, now you lie? Give me a break, Thomas."

"What do you want me to do?" He smiled. "If everyone suddenly orders a twist of lime in their water, someone's gotta go slice that citrus." He rested his elbows on his knees and cleared his throat. "Hey, you can bake. How about a job?"

Working for Tom? "Is this nepotism?" Em asked. "Are we doing nepotism?"

He smiled. "No, that's different. We're doing

frantically-trying-to-hire-qualified-employees."

"Careful what you wish for." She squinted at him. "I do need a job to tie me over." Acting alone wouldn't pay the rent.

"You do? Oh." He studied his sneakers. "I thought you were going to be a teacher."

"It's a good idea. At least I thought it was. But now I'm afraid it'll be another med school experience. I'll start just to find out I hate it."

"Your mom's a teacher," Tom said. "You know about the job. That's different from going for thoracic whatsitsname."

"Well..." Em laughed, a little ashamed for being disloyal. Her mother's job had kept the family comfortable enough. "Maybe I know too much about teaching? I don't know. I thought I wanted to do it, but I'm not so sure anymore." She didn't want to become trapped like her mom. No kids. No teaching.

"You need to settle on something." Tom ran his hand through his hair. "Figure out what you love to do."

"I know, Sherlock." Em pulled her bag on her lap. "What can I say? I think I love something, and next time I look, I've grown tired of it. Especially if it makes any sense or money." Her gaze landed on the brownstone. She needed to get going. "By the way, Regina's got a place for me." She pointed at the apartments. "I'm desperate to get out of my parents' house."

"That bad, huh?" He chuckled about echoing her words. But when Em turned, Tom was frowning at the building.

She tilted her head. "Yep. Um. Little warning, the apartment's next to yours. I can see into your kitchen from my kitchen. Not sure if it's too close for comfort?"

He looked at her silently, long enough to make her stomach sink. Who wanted their little sister living next door?

"Bit close," he said finally.

"Sorry. I'd back off if there was anything else to rent. Only there isn't, so you'll have to put up with me." Em stood and patted the dust off her jeans. "If you're serious about giving me a job... I *can* bake. I promise to get curtains and never tell your mom when you don't do your dishes. Spit twice and die."

"You better do get curtains, or I'll check on *your* dishes. And I'm telling on you, too." Tom pulled Em into a hug. "You can start tomorrow if *you're* serious."

"Wow. For real?" Her voice muffled into his chest.

"For real." He squinted down at her. "Just one thing, Em."

"Yes. What?"

"I need you to stick around. You can't suddenly quit and leave me hanging. At least not until after Christmas."

Em nodded. She wasn't actually a quitter. Or maybe she was; sometimes she wasn't so sure anymore. But she could do anything until Christmas if it paid the rent. "I promise, Tom. Count me in."

He nodded back, once, and then he kissed the top of her head and let her go. "See you tomorrow morning at seven. We open at ten."

Excitement blew air into Em's lungs, and she huffed it back out. "I'll be there."

Tom took a few steps toward the Café, walking backward, still keeping her in his sight. Then he stopped. "I had to pay a deposit for my apartment. Do you have enough?" He didn't wait for an answer. "When do you need it?"

"Tonight." Em pulled out her phone to check the time.

"What are you going to do?"

She shrugged, uncomfortable. "Not sure." Maybe she could pawn her flute. It'd been her graduation present and was easily worth the deposit. Dad could never find out if she wanted to live, and it was a really shabby thing to do, but Claire was more important.

"I gotta go, Tom. Lots to do."

"I can give you the deposit," he said quickly. "It's no problem. You'll make it back in tips the first couple of months."

"What?" Em felt lightheaded. "Really?" Then she snapped her mouth shut. "Tom, the kitchen doesn't even get tips."

"They do, too," Tom said. "Tips are good when the food's good, so we share."

"Is that true, or are you just being nice? I don't want to borrow money from you."

"Would that be so terrible?"

Em wrapped her arms around herself. "You're the only one I've got left." It sounded dramatic. But it also was how she felt. Hastily, she continued. "I don't want money to come between us."

"A thousand dollars couldn't come between us if they tried." He smiled. "The Café is doing well, Em. We played catch-up in the spring, but it's been great all summer. It's fine. I promise."

The Café *was* bursting at the seams every single day. Even the locals had caught on to Tom's cooking.

"I think what *could* come between us is you living at home." Tom took another step back, hands in pockets. "I can never catch you on your own anymore."

Em remembered the cigarettes. "We definitely need to hang out more."

"So it's a yes?"

Em mouthed an embarrassed *thank you*.

He waved her to come with him. "Call Regina before she shows the apartment to someone else."

"Okay. Oh, wow. For real, Tom." Em pulled out her cell and swiped as she walked toward him.

Tom's eyes held hers. Em's stomach started to tingle with relief, the beginning of a happy wave she knew would sweep her away if only... "Regina?" Her voice sounded high and breathless. "I have the deposit! Can I sign the contract?"

Tom gave her two thumbs-up.

Em pressed the mic to her chest. "Now or later she wants to know."

"Now. We just need to stop at the Café first."

"Now, please," Em answered into the phone, still looking into his eyes. "I'll come over right now. Okay. Thanks! Thank you."

And then the wave of joy smashed into her, a real white-crested breaker that swept her into Tom's arms, made her kiss his cheeks and throttle him in a hug that had him laugh out loud.

Chapter 8

"You did what now?" Cate stopped her chair on the back porch. The rocking chair was her favorite, a gift from her first-ever graduating class, but it creaked. Maybe she'd heard wrong. It was impossible to snag a brownstone apartment without the right connections. Ellie had told Cate all about it after Tom got his.

"It's true, Mom." Em reached for Cate's hand. Cate saw her glance at it, taking in the brown stains from peeling potatoes earlier. Em gripped it tighter.

"I signed the contract, and Regina said the owner's fine with me moving in a few days before the lease starts. Tomorrow, if I can sort out the utilities." She paused. "You aren't mad, are you?"

Cate returned the squeeze. "Of course I'm not mad, sweetheart. I think it's great." The words came from the bottom of her heart. She was lucky if Em stayed in Beach Cove at all. For a while, she'd talked about going inland to teach. "Only..."

"Only what?"

"Only I can't pay for it just now. I don't get a full salary while I'm on sabbatical."

Allen put his income into a separate account, and Cate didn't have access. He wasn't going to pay for Em's apartment because he was still angry at her. Cate had meant to straighten things out with Allen this summer, but so far, it hadn't happened. She didn't have the courage to start.

"Mom?" Em's lips were pressed tight. "Hey, it's okay. I have a new job. I can pay for the apartment."

"What job is that, Em?" Cate tried to sound casual.

"Tom's hired me at the Corner Café."

Cate chose her next words carefully. "That's fabulous," she said with as much sincerity as she could muster. It wasn't much, because Em needed Tom as a friend. He was her rock. She could still talk with Tom even when talking with Cate became too hard. Besides being Em's age, Tom had the advantage of not being married to Allen.

If Em and Tom had a falling out at work, the bit of blue sky left over Em's head would fall and crush her.

Em sighed. "What, Mom? Tell me."

"Are you sure you're going to be okay with Tom as your boss? I'm worried something will happen to your friendship if you work for him." Honesty had always been the shortest way to the heart of her children. Cate knew when she opened up, the girls did, too.

"I'll keep work and friendship separate," Em said. "I'll stay in my corner, doing my thing. I won't get under his feet."

"Good," Cate said, but when she looked at her daughter, she thought not for the first time that Tom might be the one who'd leave his corner. Both her girls were lucky mixes of Cate's curves and Allen's angles. Slim blondes with tan shoulders, long legs and intelligent eyes.

Em narrowed hers. "I don't think Tom fancies me, Mom," she said.

"He definitely might, sweetheart." How could she be so smart and yet so—

Em smiled. "I'm pretty sure Tom likes men."

Cate rocked back in surprise. "Oh, he does?" That one had never occurred to her.

"Well, think about it." Em picked a daisy that grew by her chair. "He's never had a girlfriend, has he?"

"What about... What was her name, the cute brunette with the braces?"

"Sandra?" Em laughed, and Cate was glad to see it. Her eldest didn't laugh much anymore. "That was in middle school, Mom. What, like seventh grade?"

"Yeah, Sandra. What happened to her?"

"Uh... She moved to Minneapolis to study astrology or something."

"Astronomy?"

"No, actual astrology. With some lady who was on TV reading cards. But Tom didn't ever date-date Sandra. Not in middle school. They hung out a couple of times, went for ice cream." She paused. "The only time I think he might've crushed on a girl was in high school. He never told me about it, though."

"Who was it?"

Em scrunched her nose. "Brandie Sagartati."

"Bonnie's kid? Huh." Bonnie was so strange. Her daughter probably had her own set of unique traits.

"Don't you remember her?" Em rolled her eyes.

Not because of Brandie, Cate knew. The two had been friends. The roll was probably for Cate herself. She'd missed something obvious. "Of course I do. She was a bit wild."

"Brandie was drop-dead gorgeous. All the boys wanted to date her from second grade on. By high school, they'd worked themselves in a proper frenzy."

"And she picked Alex." Handsome and wealthy, Alex had very much been the local heartbreak. Em always said he'd had his pick, but maybe Cate had underestimated how proud he'd been to date Brandie.

Alex had certainly taken their breakup hard. Hard enough to walk and walk until thirst made him eat wild grapes. Only they hadn't been grapes.

"Yeah, she did pick him. One way or the other, it wasn't easy on the boys." Em frowned at her hands.

"What do you mean, one way or the other?"

"Tom either fancied Brandie himself, or he fancied Alex," Em said quietly. "Hanging out wasn't the same once Alex and Brandie came as a package. It made everything more difficult."

"And...after?" Cate asked.

"After..." Em frowned. "After, Tom felt he should've been there for Alex when Brandie broke up with him. He thinks if things between them had been better, Alex would've come to him instead of going off on his own. It would've changed everything."

Cate gripped her arm rests. So much went on in

their kids' world they knew nothing about. For years, Tom had thought he was to blame, and maybe he'd even been in love with Alex. She needed to tell Ellie.

"Don't tell Ellie," Em said. "Not our news to share, Mom."

"I think she should know," Cate said. "I think it would help."

"Nothing helps," Em said. "How can it? Alex is dead. And Tom can tell his mom himself if he wants. He doesn't need us to do it for him."

"Okay. Good." Cate might tell Ellie anyway. Just in case.

"Ugh." Em stretched. "I'll never tell you anything again."

Cate drummed her fingers. "You realize Tom's apartment is in the brownstone?"

"He's in the other one." The corners of Em's mouth dropped as if she'd been unfairly attacked. "All the Beach Cove rental apartments are in, or right next to, Tom's building. The town isn't that big."

"Come on now, it's a little bigger than that. But who knows? Maybe it'll be nice to live so close to a friend." Cate tried to sound optimistic. They'd been friends this long. Maybe it'd be okay to also work and practically live together.

Em glanced at her. "It's not like I get to choose, Mom. But I don't mind. I had to promise him I wouldn't stare into his kitchen, though."

"It'll be all right." Cate wanted to make amends for her skepticism. It was best not to put a flea in Em's ear. So far, so good. "You forever hang out anyway."

"Not since he's running the Café. He's barely ever got time anymore." Em scratched her chin. "I'd like to show you the new place tomorrow. Can I borrow the vacuum?"

Cate waited a few moments before she answered, so her tone would be cheerful. She still had Claire for a short while. "You can have the yellow vacuum if you like; I never use it. Take the box with the cleaning supplies, too. I just washed all your sheets and the duvet. Do you want help packing?" Most of Em's things were stowed in the basement, in the same few boxes she'd brought back from med school. Cate knew Em didn't need her to shift them, but maybe she could drive a few loads for her daughter.

"I'd love some help." Em smiled at Cate, a quick acknowledgment that yes, she wanted Cate to be there for the start of her new life. "Thanks, Mom."

Cate tucked a strand of her daughter's blond hair back. "Anytime, my dear."

Chapter 9

"I like it. Very much." Vince, Maisie's neighbor, nodded his approval. "It looks Grecian."

"I like it too." Maisie frowned, still critical about the change. The wall to Robert's old office was gone. A wide arch now opened the re-purposed room to the rest of the house, showing off the new built-in bookshelves. Light fell through the tall windows, filtered by sweeping white curtains. Outside, the street meandered like a creek through the purple heather toward the village. No view of the sea on this side of the house, but it was still pretty. Inn guests would enjoy reading here on rainy days.

Vince crossed his hands behind his back. His shoulders were slightly hunched, his eyes carefully lidded.

"I can't believe you're seeing it for the first time." Maisie wanted to put a hand on his arm. Connect somehow, get the eyes to open up and look at her. "When were you last here?" It was fall, and his apple orchard seemed as demanding as a hungry toddler.

"Not since we stocked the shelves." He glanced at her, and Maisie almost thought he'd winked. But it was hard to tell. "I had no idea you were going to take out the wall," he said. "I like it very much indeed. And those curtains are marvelous." He smiled, as if he'd made a little joke.

"I put them up weeks ago." Of course, it wasn't just the apples keeping Vince away. She knew it was her fault he didn't visit more often.

She hadn't reacted well to Vince's accidental kiss on the bench by the ocean. The feel of his lips on hers had confused Maisie. Then she'd realized because she'd finally found Alex, she now had space to sort out her feelings for Robert. It was the next step necessary to heal.

She took the time to feel her way forward and discovered her sense of loyalty to the old marriage had dissolved. She understood why Robert had ended his life, but she also knew he'd consciously let her go. And after a decade of bitter loneliness, Maisie had let go of Robert, too. She was ready to move on.

However, she probably shouldn't kiss her charming neighbor until she at least knew if he was a harmless retiree or the banished head of a *famiglia*.

Even Vince's nationality wasn't clear. While he preferred a British accent and claimed to be a Londoner, he spoke several languages fluently. He also had an uncanny ability to change his appearance with the tilt of a shoulder or the drop of his chin.

There'd been abruptly ended calls when she'd walked in, papers hastily slipped under international newspapers, silence around strangers.

"Well, if you've seen enough, we might go

outside," Maisie suggested. "It's a beautiful morning, and the asters are blooming." They could chat a little, catch up and rebuild the familiarity the kiss had cost them.

"That sounds lovely. By the way, how are the guestrooms? You have put such effort into them."

"We overcame all obstacles and hung the last picture yesterday."

"I'm glad to hear it. Congratulations."

"Thanks." Maisie smiled. "Would you like to see?"

"I certainly would." Vince smiled back. "The captain who built the house was an interesting old chap. In fact, I'd love to see the entire house sometime."

"And I'd love to show you." Maisie faintly remembered long ago promising a tour. She quickly ran through her plans for the day. Planting the peony bulbs could wait. "Do you have time right now?"

"I do."

"Well, how about..." She looked around. "You do know the ground level, of course."

"Yes, I believe so." He waited while she thought about possible touring routes.

"How about we start upstairs? That's where our bedrooms are, and uh, some hallways."

Vince tilted his head. "I'd hate to disturb your privacy."

"It's okay. I've made my bed," Maisie tried to joke.

"I'm sure you have." He raised an eyebrow but quickly dropped it again. "However, let's work our way from the bottom up. Is it true the basement is dug into rock?"

She stopped. "You want to see the *basement*?" She barely ever put a foot down there. Not if she could help it. "What's to see besides cobwebs and rafters?"

"I don't know," he responded. "Nothing at all, I suppose. But how often does one get to see a basement built by a mad captain?"

Maisie leaned forward as if she hadn't caught the words. "Why mad? Mad how?"

"Oh." Vince lifted an eyebrow. "He was an odd fish, wasn't he? At least that's how the story goes."

Maisie closed her eyes, annoyed. She'd never heard a story about the captain having been mad. Or odd. She'd spent hours researching the house and its history and considered herself an expert.

As far as the official record, the captain had invested his hard-earned money and made a fortune, then settled down with a much younger wife to raise a bunch of perfectly spoiled kids. It really had seemed very straightforward.

But Vince always knew more. It must be all the old books he bought at Sam's. Then again, Maisie, too, had bought her books at Sam's.

"Where did you hear this?" she asked after she'd opened her eyes again.

"Here or there." Vince shrugged. "I can't remember."

Maisie sighed and led the way to the basement door. "At least tell me the story, Vince. What sort of mad?"

"Well, he appears to have been a bit of a pirate.

A number of ships that should've crossed his routes disappeared, never to be found. At the same time, his wealth grew very much in proportion to the value of the lost cargo."

"Ah, that sort of mad." Maisie opened the door to the basement. The hinge creaked. Without good reason, as far she could see. It was new. "And here I thought the captain was a clever old man who'd invested his hard-earned money wisely. It's never that easy, is it?" She started down the narrow staircase, groping the rough wall for the light switch. The air smelled dank, and she blew out a breath.

"I'm afraid he wasn't very nice." It was Vince who flicked the light on. "Though he did love his wife."

"Oh good. Yes?"

"In a way."

"And what is that supposed to mean?"

Like the intestines of a whale, the stairs wound long and moist into the depth. Maisie now remembered that she hated the stairs. The basement, too. She wanted to have coffee on the patio or plant peonies. She'd even discuss the aesthetic of yellow curtains one more time if it meant she could go back upstairs.

"That means he quite possibly hadn't been taught how to express his feelings in appropriate ways. Love included," Vince said behind her. "Next time, I should probably go first, my dear. The steps are a bit slippery."

They'd reached the bottom. Maisie stepped on the dirt floor; she could feel the cool of it seep through the soles of her espadrilles. Shivering, she rubbed her arms.

Vince shrugged out of his linen jacket and draped it over her shoulders. "That dress is far too pretty to go spelunking," he remarked cheerfully.

Maisie pulled the jacket tight; it smelled of Vince, of olive bread and oil paints and the tea he brewed in the kitchen of Carriage House. "Thank you," she said sincerely. "So...well, this is it. The basement." She peered into the gloom. The staircase light illuminated a small circle where they stood, but vaulted rooms stretched far into the dark.

"Very nice," Vince muttered and took a few steps toward the void.

"Uh, and so...what did he do to his wife?" Maisie asked, putting a hand on the railing to make sure the staircase didn't vanish.

Vince took another step into the dark. "She disappeared too, didn't she?"

"She did?" Maisie asked weakly.

"Well, yes." She couldn't see him anymore; there was only his voice. "And she was never found either."

"Are you checking whether he buried her down here?" she called after him.

"Of course not," he said. "But it'll take me a moment if that's all right. No need to wait if you'd rather not."

"I'll be on the patio." She put her foot on the bottom stair. "In the sunshine, where the flowers are. Looking at the blue sky, drinking hot coffee and eating sweet crumb cake. My grandma's recipe, clipped from a normal housekeeping magazine and kept safe.

Because my grandma cared about things. People, too. She was very caring."

"That sounds lovely," came the echo. "I'll only just have a quick look around. Be right up."

———————◆◆———————

Maisie was drinking her second cup of sugary coffee when she heard Vince open the door to the patio.

"And?" She turned her face into the sun, soaking up the heat. "Done with your ghoulish investigation?"

"Do you realize how many rooms there are in the basement?" He came to stand beside her.

"I've never counted. I've never been in all of them, either. In fact, I avoid going down there. It's like a dungeon." She shivered.

"I agree. Quite unpleasant." Vince poured himself a cup from the carafe and sat. "It might help if I set up a few mouse traps. You don't want any pests to come upstairs in the winter."

"Oh. Okay." Maisie sat up. It sounded like quite the infestation. "Traps would be great. Thanks."

Vince sipped his brew, looking lost in thought. "You don't mind if I drop by regularly to check the traps? I know we haven't— But you wouldn't want to leave a catch sitting too long."

Maisie tried not to picture it. "Ew, no. You're welcome to check as often as you like." She'd see Vince more often too. At least until the mice were gone. "Maybe let's wrap up the tour with the guestrooms?"

"Let's." Vince pulled on the jacket she handed him,

and they went back inside.

Maisie chatted, pointed out this and that improvement on the way, the five bedrooms and sitting rooms, all of which Vince seemed to like. She made him sit in the new armchairs to get his opinion —Ellie said they were too soft—and help her level a crooked nightstand.

"One of my old friends called me last night," he mentioned on the way back. "He'd like to visit if you'll have him."

"The inn is ready," Maisie said. They entered the entrance hall. "Your friend is welcome to pick a room."

Vince nodded. "May I bring him over Thursday?"

Maisie took a breath to steady her nerves. She'd hosted endless guests for Robert, but she was out of practice. Opening her own little inn gave her stage fright. "Yes, Thursday's great. I'll let Ellie know so we're ready for action."

"Not much action required on your part, I'm sure. He'll adore the inn just as it is." Vince opened the front door. "He'll adore you and Ellie even more." He hesitated for a moment, and Maisie thought he was going to turn. But he only said over his shoulder, "I'll set up the traps this afternoon if you don't mind," and stepped outside.

"Wait." Maisie went to the sideboard and fished a spare key from the drawer. She'd made extras for future guests, and Vince might as well have one too.

"The basement is all yours. Come whenever you like." Maisie handed him the key with a smile, wondering whether Vince knew the basement was rumored to tunnel under the village and into the coast.

Vince took the key with a little bow and a promise to keep it safe. Tucking it into his shirt pocket, he left.

Maisie watched him walk away. Then she shut the door and leaned against it. His scent still enveloped her, a fragrance as smart as the man himself.

"Secret agent," Maisie whispered into the sudden quiet of the house. "Please just be a nice, normal, retired secret agent."

Chapter 10

The golden bell over the bookstore's entrance jingled.

Sam looked up. She'd been pricing books, researching editions on the internet and hunching over covers to pencil in dollar amounts. Her neck was stiff. She massaged it to loosen the cramped muscles. "Bonnie?"

Bonnie nodded. Her red hair wasn't bunched under an old cap as usual but streamed over her shoulders. As if it were underwater, it seemed to move with a will of its own.

"Sam Burrow." Bonnie's voice had no expression, no feeling, no nothing.

Sam rearranged her features into something welcoming. It was Bowers, not Burrow. Burrow was the name of Sam's ancestor Sally, whose claim to fame was a hasty escape from the Salem witch trials. Sally's last name had long ago been lost to marriage.

Sam had told Bonnie. Several times.

"Uh, hi. Come on in." Sam closed her laptop warily. When Bonnie was near, Sam's skin started to prickle. She was tempted to rub her arms, flatten the little hairs that tingled with static energy.

Bonnie had only once come to the store. She'd searched the shelves for a long time without finding a book. In the end, Sam had handed Bonnie the thriller she'd been reading herself, just to get rid of the woman.

"Can I help you with something, Bonnie?" Sam expected Bonnie to shake her head. But she didn't even get that much.

Bonnie was a fisherwoman in a town full of fishermen. Fishing was a tough business. Sam couldn't imagine how it must be for a woman. With white skin that never burned or tanned, a shock of fiery locks clashing with mossy green irises, and a figure that turned oilskins into couture, the woman was beautiful. Exceptionally, wildly.

It was no use Bonnie hid in grimy jeans and baggy hoodies, knit caps and clunky work boots. Her beauty burned too bright. Women wished they knew her secrets. Men who didn't know Bonnie stumbled over their feet to catch another glimpse.

Men who did know her used their feet to change sidewalks instead. Bonnie didn't mind bringing home a man now and then, but Sam thought it was strictly on her terms. Stories had a way of getting around in small towns.

"You know," Sam said suddenly, "your hair is really beautiful."

Bonnie still stood by the door. She jerked her head at the store window. "The sun's shining, but it's dark in here."

"I know. I know." The eyes needed time to adjust

to the dim store, and Sam had gotten these comments before. "It doesn't matter how many lamps I bring in. It's the books; they eat all the light. Sometimes more, sometimes less. They do what they want."

Bonnie turned to the shelves. "They do what they want?"

Sam bit the inside corner of her mouth, embarrassed. To her, the books felt like living things. Right now, they cowered in their shelves, practically putting their arms over their heads to hide.

Of course books had no arms. Or heads. All the shifting and shuffling was strictly in Sam's imagination: feelings projected on inanimate objects. Sam knew that. Everyone knew that.

"Not literally, of course." Unfortunately, Bonnie had no sense of humor at all. Not one whimsical bone. "I mean, they *do* swallow light, but it's always the same amount. Because...I guess it must be? Same number of pages, am I right?"

Unsmiling, Bonnie took a step toward her, lithe as a stalking panther.

Sam slid off her stool. She'd rather face Sagartati standing. The closer the woman came, the stronger became her scent. Sam's nostrils flared involuntarily. A mix of rotting shell and diesel fuel, sea tar, drying tidepool.

She turned her head aside for a gasp of clean air. "Coming straight from the boat?"

"No," Bonnie said and put her hands on the counter.

The next breath Sam took smelled of cheap

shampoo and dryer sheets. Scents to camouflage everything and everyone. A relief, but also spooky. Sam sniffed the air again, and again Bonnie smelled like any other customer. Where had the marine stench come from? Sam glanced over her shoulder, then under the counter. Was she going crazy?

"Okay, then." She forced herself to sound cheerful. "What's up, Bonnie? Looking for your next interesting read?"

"Do you have one for me, Sam Burrow?" Bonnie asked, her green eyes locked on Sam's. "A book of interest?"

"No, not really." Sam cursed herself silently for asking. She knew what Bonnie wanted.

Last time, she'd sucked like an octopus onto Sam's newly inherited books. The old family cookbook in particular. Handwritten by generations of women, with comments scribbled in the margins, it had recently fallen from Mimi to Sam.

The book wasn't old enough to be worth a ton of money. But to Sam, it had tremendous value as an addition to her tiny collection, since she already owned Sally's cookbook. The founding mother had smuggled her recipes out of witch-frenzied Salem and carried them all the way to Beach Cove.

None of the recipes in the ancestral collection were tasty. Sam had tried a bunch and tossed the results without exception. But it wasn't about the recipes. It was the fact that woman after woman had handled the book, charging it with their thoughts, their time, the vibrations of their lives.

Sam couldn't explain the power these female books held over her, but she wasn't about to let anyone sap their magic. She certainly wasn't going to let anyone touch the books. And she certainly *certainly* wasn't going to let Bonnie touch them. In case of fire or flood, Maisie maybe. Cate, maybe. Ellie might drop them.

"I don't have anything interesting for you," Sam repeated.

"No. You don't." Bonnie's eyes detached from Sam's face like bored limpets.

Sam's stomach dropped with relief. Bonnie was weird at the best of times. But those sea-lettuce eyes without a glint of feeling gave Sam the shivers.

It didn't help to know that Ellie's ex-husband Dale had developed an unhealthy passion for the beautiful fisherwoman. Unhealthy, because Bonnie had lured Dale onto her lobster boat under false pretense and left him without means of getting back.

She'd never said how long he'd been trapped. But they knew it'd been long enough to stop his unwanted attention. Desperate, Dale had eventually broken out of the boat's belly, jumped into the sea and swam to land. He'd sulked a few months and then left town.

Sam didn't blame Bonnie. She'd never liked Dale either. But it was unnerving how unapologetic the fisherwoman was about kidnapping people who got on her nerves.

"Uh, anything else I can do for you?" Sam's hands were damp. She wiped them on her jeans, hoping Bonnie wouldn't notice.

"I'm returning your book." Bonnie reached into the kangaroo pocket of her hoodie and pulled out the thriller she'd taken last time. The pages crinkled as if she'd read it in the bathtub.

"Oh!" Sam didn't know what to say. She'd been sure she'd never see the copy again. "You didn't have to do that. You could've kept it."

"The man dies." Bonnie laid the paperback on the counter. "He dies badly."

Sam looked at it. Were there good ways to die? "Spoiler alert, huh?"

Bonnie tilted her chin up. "How are you, Sam?"

"How am I?" The question felt as foreign as a finger in the eye. "Um. I'm good. How are you, Bonnie?"

"No. How are *you*?" Bonnie lowered her head, but not her eyes. Like a mother warning a child not to be dim.

"Right." Sam sighed. "Well, I'm good. I...uh...I don't know what else to say. It's nice outside. Nice weather. Nice fall."

Bonnie stared and after a charged minute, Sam was ready to swear the woman had trained as a professional interrogator. Did she never have to blink? Sam scraped her brain. "My husband's traveling," she finally tossed out. "He's in Turkey."

"Yes." Bonnie's eyes shifted into a darker shade. "Your husband, Larry. What is he doing in Turkey?"

Sam tried to slip into the easy chatter she used with her customers. "He's researching some old manuscripts. So fun." It wasn't exactly a secret. Larry liked to talk about his work, and a lot of Beach Covians knew more about Middle Eastern lore than they cared for.

"Manuscripts about what?"

Sam tilted her head. Bonnie was a lot smarter than people gave her credit for. Sam knew Bonnie could put two and two together. Sam also knew Bonnie read, though not books from her store.

"He'll have to find out. That's his job. I only know the scrolls were found in Syria." She cleared her throat. "Can you imagine?"

Bonnie ignored the question. "Where in Syria? What town?"

"What *town*?" Sam stared. "I have no idea, Bonnie. Somewhere at the coast."

"And now Larry's in Turkey. Where exactly? Also at the coast?"

Üzem İskelesi, a tiny town with few houses and even fewer people. But it wasn't any of the fisherwoman's business. Sam cleared her throat. "Yep, he's somewhere at the coast." She tapped a finger on the returned paperback. "So how does it end?"

Bonnie lifted an eyebrow. "I already told you, Sam. It ends badly."

Chapter 11

By the time Sam walked up the garden path to her Victorian, the evening washed the sky with swaths of lavender and mauve. And by the time she entered the house and locked the front door twice behind her, Sam was ready to get on the phone and vent to a friend.

"She said it all ends badly? That's pretty gloom and doom." Maisie sounded breathless. Sam figured she was either washing rugs, polishing silver or kneading dough.

Sam rolled her eyes. "Who knows with that woman?"

"Are you sure she was talking about the book? It almost sounds like a veiled threat."

Sam had considered it. "I don't know. I don't want to believe she's got a reason since I've done nothing to deserve threats. I don't even know why she came to the store. What does she want from me?"

"I thought she returned the book. The thriller?"

"That was only a decoy. An excuse to come to the store." Sam felt sure of it.

Maisie clicked her tongue. "Or maybe you're imagining things. Bonnie makes me see things too.

You should've been inside her trailer that one time; I was so scared I could barely see straight."

"You said things were shifting."

"I must've been dizzied with fear." Maisie gave an unconvincing laugh. "But it was silly of me. We all made it out alive, even Ellie. And I think it's nice Bonnie returned the book."

"I don't want it anymore. It's ruined. The paper got wet and dried all frilly. I hate that."

Maisie chuckled. "More gloom and doom."

Sam huffed. "You know what? She did ask me something specific."

"Let's have it."

"She wanted to know about Larry and his research. Where he was exactly, like the name of the town. I didn't give it to her. She's way too interested in him if you know what I mean." Sam frowned at the wall. It wasn't so long since Ellie found out about Bonnie and Dale.

"Aww, come on, Sam." Maisie chuckled. "Not *Larry*. He's not the type."

"He's attractive enough, Maisie," Sam muttered. "Only he works too much." Larry wasn't interested in romance; she knew that from years of first-hand experience. He was interested in his research.

"Maybe she wants to know about the manuscripts," Maisie joked. "Maybe she's interested in scooping his publication and get her paper in first."

"Why on earth would Bonnie be interested in old manuscripts?" Sam asked.

"Ellie!" Maisie called suddenly. "The window

cleaner is here! Could you get the door, please?"

"Ugh." Sam rubbed her ear. "I'll let you go. Sounds like you're busy."

"Sorry, Sam," Maisie said at a normal volume. "Our first guest arrives tomorrow. We're scrambling to get ready."

"The inn's been ready for months. The inn was ready before you knew you wanted an inn."

"Not true."

"Perfectionism is a curse, my dear. Hey, the guy that's going to stay with you—you said he's Vince's friend. Do you know anything about him?"

"You mean Vince?" Maisie asked wryly. "Or his friend? The answer would be no in either case."

"True." Sam laughed at Maisie's frustration. "I barely know Vince lives in Carriage House, and he's my best customer. Maybe he's one of those sociopaths, Maisie. You have to yawn in front of him. It's a test. Sociopaths don't pick up on a yawn because they're monsters that don't speak human." She grinned. She liked Vince. They all liked Vince. But Maisie deserved some teasing for saying Larry wasn't attractive. "Don't kiss yet! Unless it's too late already? Have you two... uh..."

"Don't be silly, Sam. I do have to go. Ellie's waving papers at me, and I'd better—"

Sam could hear Ellie's muffled voice calling. "Bye, Maisie," she said. "As soon as your guest gets there, let me know."

"Why? What are you planning to do?" Maisie sounded alarmed.

"I don't know. I might stop by, have a quick look at him, say hi. He's going to stay at your house, after all. Can't be too careful."

"Oh. Uh. I don't know, Sam. Is that a good idea?"

Sam frowned. "Here's a good idea, Maisie. If he gets his pants in a knot just because I show up and say hi, you might get rid of him whether or not he's safe."

Maisie made a small sound, something between a laugh and a sigh. "I'm sorry, my dear. Stop by whenever you feel like it. Of course you can come have a look."

"That's my girl," Sam said. "With that attitude, he'll have a hard time getting you to join his cult."

"I don't think Vince's going to invite cult leaders into Beach House," Maisie said mildly. "If he does, there'll be trouble. And I think he likes not being in trouble. He's developed flying under the radar into a fine art."

Paper rustled. Sam didn't want to let Maisie go, but clearly, she was needed elsewhere. "I've got to go. I too have very important things to do."

"Bye, Sam," Maisie said without acknowledging Sam's little joke. In the background, Ellie started talking.

Sam ended the call, feeling left out.

It was unreasonable to feel like that, she realized. Maisie was nervous over the pending arrival of the inn's first guest, and she'd pulled Ellie into the maelstrom.

It was very quiet in the living room. Very dark. Sam switched on the lights, and then dialed Cate's number. Cate didn't answer, so Sam tossed the phone on the couch and strolled into the kitchen to check the contents of the fridge. There was an open bottle of pinot in there, some leftover ratatouille, a jar of syrup plums some student had gifted Larry. Not exactly a match made in heaven, but Sam decided to have all three, and plenty.

Sam shoved her plate into the microwave, wondering if Cate was busy too. Probably not. Probably she was sitting in the yard, enjoying Allen's absence.

It was a pity Bonnie hadn't locked Allen on her boat. In the race for worst husband, Allen was so far ahead, the dust on the track had settled and fossilized by the time Dale came trotting along.

The microwave dinged, interrupting Sam's thoughts. She prodded the heaping rice with a fork. A little dry but good enough. She brought what she needed to the fireplace and lit a fire with the last of the wood Larry had stacked. Then she poured herself a glass and snuggled into the armchair.

But it wasn't cozy. The lumbar pillow was too stiff. When she pulled it out, her back slouched. And now Sam didn't want the food anymore either. The plums likely belonged into cocktails anyway. She pushed the plate onto the coffee table and took a sip of wine. And another.

She'd call Larry. He should've arrived. He should've called too, but he was no doubt busy and not thinking of her sitting in Beach Cove, worrying. It was important to stay in touch. Larry wasn't going to do it on his own, naturally. Keeping in touch would be her job.

Sam took a proper drink and topped up her glass. Then she copied the string of numbers he'd sent in an email and tapped dial.

"Sam? Why are you calling me?" Larry's voice was distant and more than a little annoyed.

Sam frowned. "You should've called *me* when you arrived," she snapped. She'd wanted to connect with her husband. Maybe get a little comfort. Not this.

Static buzzed as if Larry was changing location. "Sorry, kid," he whispered suddenly. It was hard to understand him through the crackle. "It's been a long trip. I've had no sleep at all."

"Are you safe?" Sam was still irritated—even tired, he shouldn't be annoyed with her.

"Of course," Larry said, but he spoke through the nose. Larry only spoke through the nose when he wasn't truthful. It made him sound affected, like a bad actor playing a liar on stage.

Sam emptied her glass. Why was he lying about being safe? "Tell me at once what's going on," she ordered. "Are you in Üzem İskelesi? Are you with Patrick?"

Patrick was the keeper of the smuggled manuscripts. Sam had automatically assumed the name was a cover when Larry told her, because how likely was it an Irish smuggler brought Syrian documents to Turkey? Then again, now that she thought about it, of course it was possible the Irish liked Turkey's sunny coast well enough. Any crowd harbored the random smuggler. It was also possible there was a crowd of smugglers, with the random Irish person mixed in. Anything was possible. Sam refilled her glass. There was still more left in the bottle, though.

"Are you with Patrick?" she repeated. Normally, Sam didn't begrudge Larry his Indiana Jones moments. But normally, Larry didn't lie through his nose about being safe.

"Well, no. It turned out that... Never mind, Sammy. I'll email you the story sometime, but it's very boring and all about flight delays. Listen, I've got to go and have dinner with some people, okay? I'll call you when I have a minute. It might take a few days, so please don't freak out."

Sam pulled her chin back. "I never freak out."

"I know, I know," Larry said hastily. "I'll call, Sammy. Love you. Hang in there." He ended the call.

"What the..." Sam stared at her phone as if it'd turned into a can of peas, then tossed it back on the coffee table and drained her glass.

He'd lied about being safe. He wasn't where he was supposed to be.

Had Patrick materialized? Was Patrick even real?

Sam replenished her glass and leaned back to watch the dying fire. "Wait a moment," she muttered after a few minutes. "You're not having dinner at all."

She tried to calculate the time difference in her head, then gave up and googled it. It was 10 a.m. in Turkey. *Morning.* Yet Larry had begged off the call claiming he was expected at dinner. A dinner with people.

"What's going on?" Sam murmured at the embers. "Where is he really?"

Just then the phone rang, jumping like a poltergeist.

Sam lunged for it. "Yes? Larry?"

"Oh. I'm awfully sorry. I'm not him, unfortunately." A male voice Sam didn't recognize.

Sam squinted at the screen. Boston area code. "Who's this?" she demanded, falling back into her chair. Pinot spilled from the glass on her T-shirt, but it was black and didn't matter.

"Dave," the man answered. "It's Dave."

Sam frowned. "Which one?" She knew at least ten Daves, but none who'd call her. And she was worried about Larry. She didn't want to talk to a Dave.

"The one with the attic inheritance scam?" Dave said apologetically. "Your distant relative from Italy? Dave Macintosh."

Sam almost dropped her red. "What?"

"Yes—hi. I'm sorry to call you out of the blue."

"*Again.*" Their first, last, and only contact had come out of the blue as well. He'd let her know she'd inherited some things from Mimi, the great-grandaunt she hadn't known existed. Had existed.

Back then, Sam figured Dave was a scammer. But the bequest turned out to be real, and Sam collected a few boxes full of miscellaneous old things from Mimi Lester's attic.

"Yes. Again. I suppose I didn't have too many options," David said good-naturedly.

"I'm sorry, Dave," Sam said, remembering the trouble he'd gone to letting her know she might be rich. "It's nice to hear your voice again. I didn't mean to bark. I'm hungry, but I don't want rice. Or veggies. I like broccoli, though."

"That's... No, I understand." He laughed, and his laugh was as nice as his voice. Genuine, as if her words had struck a funny chord. "My mom was like that too," he said, but Sam didn't know what he meant.

"How's she doing?" She set her glass on the table, squinting at the bottle. The label seemed to be slipping, and she touched a finger to it so it would stay on. Maybe she shouldn't have glugged the wine so quickly.

"Oh, you know." Dave's tone was conversational. "Still dead."

Sam squeezed her eyes shut in a flash of clarity. Of course. His mom had passed on.

During the last call, Dave had claimed her spirit wanted to say hi to Sam. She'd said hi back without giving it a second thought. Only later had it occurred to her that it might've been good to follow up.

All of a sudden, Sam felt as if a drum circle was starting in her head. A few tentative beats to get the session started. And then a real hit, mallet smashing taught skin, everything set swinging. Red wine did that to her. She pressed a finger on the spot between her eyes that was supposed to be her third eye, but it made her even dizzier. "Are you a clairvoyant, Dave?" she asked and left the spot alone. Who knew what a third eye was? Could be she didn't want to activate hers.

"Are they the ones who can see the future?" David sounded interested.

"Uh. I don't know," Sam admitted. "What are the other ones called?"

"Hmm. I think there are…hypnotists? Wait, that sounds like a circus trick."

"Yeah. Psychologists? No. Those are legit."

"No, they're…*psychics*. That's what they're called!" Dave's voice rose in triumph.

"Yes!" Psychic was correct, but Sam had forgotten why they were trying to find words. She'd pour the rest of the pinot in the ficus. The bottle had been another leftover from Larry. Larry with his syrup plums. From now on, she'd only buy white wine.

"Why are you calling?" she asked, her words lilting sideways.

"Well, I'm in the States and I'd hoped—"

Sam interrupted him, bumping into his sentence like an unsteady sailor. "I thought you didn't have money for airplane tickets." That'd been his excuse for skipping Mimi's leftovers himself. He'd said he lived in Italy and was too poor to fly across the pond.

"I borrowed it." He sighed as if there was a whole lot more to the story. "What are you doing right now, my friend?"

He'd called her his friend. Sam's mood rose a notch. Unfortunately, so did her headache. The drum circle had marched past her temples to the crown of her skull. "I'm drinking wine in front of the fire," she said weakly.

"That sounds nice," he said mildly. "A lot of wine?"

"Pinot," she confided. "I can't stomach it. It's only chardonnay from now on. The supermarket has plenty."

"I see. Well, I'll be quick, so I can let you go."

Sam didn't especially want Dave to let her go. Her friends were busy or not answering their phones, her husband was secretive and distant in all the ways, a woman with overly green eyes had sort of threatened her. Sam quite liked having Dave on the phone.

But when she looked up, the room slanted. Once. As if to threaten her. "Okay. Do be quick." Sam swallowed. "I have to go."

"I'm going to visit you," Dave said. "Soon."

"You what?" Sam rubbed a hand over her damp forehead. "I haven't invited you."

"But you're my only relative left, and we might never have another chance to meet. Just a coffee in a super public space? Please?"

Sam slouched in her chair. The last flame flickered, waving red and orange hands like a drowning demon.

Did she want Dave to come to Beach Cove? Officially, she shouldn't. He was still a stranger after all, one who'd researched her on the internet. Bit stalky, bit scammy. Her guts, however, seemed okay with the visit.

"Only one coffee," she declared. "If we don't like each other, we don't have to talk. And we can have a piece of cake too. Carrot cake."

He chuckled. "And what happens if we do like each

other? Just out of curiosity. I'm not saying we will."

"Then we can talk," Sam allowed.

"Sounds promising. So—where can I find you?"

"Oh." Sam hadn't realized Dave didn't know where she lived. Maybe he wasn't very stalky after all. "Beach Cove, in Maine. Up the coast, an hour and change from Bay Port."

"An hour and change? That's not very precise."

Sam clasped her throat. Her stomach was rebelling against the pinot, or the smell of the untouched ratatouille, or the mention of carrot cake. "No," she confirmed. "It's not. Come when you can." And then she ended the call because Dave could find her now.

Chapter 12

Cate sat in her living room, hands folded on her lap, eyes unseeing.

It'd been fun staying at Beach House. It'd been easy to spend her days how she liked. It'd been a relief not to walk on eggshells around Allen. The only difficult thing had been Helene because Helene was angry. But Helene was also disciplined, and she'd tackled Cate like an overdue project.

They'd walked on the beach, with the sea as the backdrop to their first stormy conversations. But every storm helped clear the air. At first, they couldn't even drink tea together. Later, when they were hungry, they managed to sit in the Harbor Shack and eat mussels and lobster, seafood lasagna and salmon pie. Their uneasy truce smelled of rubber boots and baked garlic, but to Cate it was as unexpected and refreshing as the Shack's lavish prosecco slushies.

They compared childhood stories. Helene to prove Cate wrong, Cate because it was her only defense. As expected, Helene knew what Mother had meant her to know. It was word against word. Helene accused, and Cate countered with one story after the other, like a magician pulling bits of the past from a black hat.

The slushies helped. Breathing helped, too.

No, she hadn't wanted Helene's inheritance. No, she hadn't stormed out of the hospital. Cate hadn't eaten Aunt Jane's muffin, kicked the cat, unraveled Mother's knitting, forged signatures, slept around.

Helene's nose wrinkled with suspicion. "I suffer from depression," she said, accusation in her voice. "I know it has to do with you."

Cate took a swig of water and one of prosecco to wash away the taste of history. "I'm sorry."

"It's hard to believe Mother treated you so badly. Maybe you're just sorry for yourself."

"That's exactly what narcissistic mothers want you to think, Helene." Cate pushed her fried clams away. She couldn't stomach food on top of the memories. "There's a playbook and a pattern. They pick a golden child to make them proud and a scapegoat to blame for what goes wrong. The golden child is absorbed. The scapegoat is cast out. We're not the only daughters this happened to."

"I don't know what to believe."

Cate knew that feeling well. It was like walking on a swaying ship and about as nauseating. It'd taken therapy and reading to steady the ground under her own feet. "The clash between what you saw and what you were told is disorienting," she said. "You know what actually happened, but Mother's version seems right because she told you it was. Your mind doesn't like that split. It needs to know the truth."

Helene speared a clam and changed track. "You

never loved her. You were never sad she died."

Cate felt her forehead crumple. "I loved her desperately; she was my mother. But I lost her much earlier than you. I had to work through the stages before she even passed away." Cate remembered the sleepless grief after realizing it wasn't self-pity or her imagination. Mother truly wanted nothing to do with her. Like all grief, it was still there. Waiting its turn.

She gripped her glass tighter. "I see mothers and daughters everywhere. I've got a radar for them, the way a woman who can't get pregnant is suddenly surrounded by moms with babies. I had to come to terms with never being good enough for my own mother." She cleared her throat. "I tried to be. I worked for it. You were there, Helene. You know."

Helene looked rebellious.

"How about you?" Cate asked. "It can't have been easy for you either, carrying all that expectation."

For a moment, Helene's features shifted into a different face. The lips loosened, and the cheeks dropped; her eyes shimmered. "No. It wasn't easy."

"I think you came here," Cate said, "because she taught you to blame me. She taught you to believe your unhappiness is my fault. But how can it be?" She rubbed her forehead. "It's been so many years since we saw each other."

Helene studied her hands. "I know," she said quietly.

Cate felt her way to the heart of Helene's pain. "Even if I'd stayed in Stoning, I couldn't have helped you," she said. "I might not be able to help you now.

Only you can decide what your reality is."

And then Cate had leaned back. Her mouth had felt dry and rough. She'd talked enough.

They'd paid, each their own dinner, and left the Shack. Helene had been silent as they'd walked to her rental car, but she'd said good night. Briefly, lightly, she'd touched Cate's arm.

Cate had gone back to Ellie and Maisie, feeling as if she'd lost weight. She'd felt lighter. She'd felt *safe*.

But now she was back in her own house because Allen had sent a text. The seminar had been cut short, and he was on his way home.

Cate shifted in her seat. Her stomach hurt; maybe she should take something to make it better.

She could make a quick run to the Beach Cove Pharmacy. Even just the store's clean eucalyptus scent would make her feel better.

Calvin would be behind his counter, looking at her with that funny dead-pan expression.

No.

Cate pressed a fist into her stomach. She could heal her marriage. She hadn't tried hard enough. She could try harder.

Outside, a car door slammed shut.

Cate drew a shallow breath. Allen would be tired. And when he was tired, he was angry.

She stood, smoothing her skirt. Allen liked her to wear skirts halfway down the calf. Not too low, because he didn't want her to look old-fashioned. And not too short either, because she didn't have the legs for it. But this skirt was good. It hid her fat legs in a stylish way.

Cate opened the front door. "Allen!" She made her voice cheerful. "How nice to see you!"

Her husband dropped his bag on the floor. There were blue shadows under his eyes, and his hair looked like he'd slept in the car. "Hi."

Cate smiled. Hi was good. Hi meant he wasn't mad. Maybe she could keep him talking. "How are you? Did you have a good time?"

He pushed the front door shut, and Cate knew right away she'd overstepped. "Stop," he said. I'm not one of your students."

"Oh, sorry." She'd not meant to sound patronizing. "Can I get you something? A glass of lemonade?" She knew it was a desperate effort, that he'd say no.

"Don't make a fuss." Allen picked up his bag and started toward the bedroom. "I need some quiet if it's not asking too much."

Suddenly, unexpectedly, something snapped in Cate. Some rubber band that had kept her together. She knew she should wait until he'd showered and eaten, until he was in a better mood. But her muscles moved on their own, making her step in his way, blocking his way to the bedroom.

Allen's eyebrows rose.

"We have to talk." Her voice pitched with stress. "You can't treat me like this." She thought he'd ignore her, walk around her without a word, make her pay later. "I won't allow it."

He shook his head. "What are you going to do about it?"

"I'm going to leave you." The words came out of nowhere. She'd not meant to say them. More. She'd meant to *not* say them.

Cate felt dizzy, as if she was about to faint. Her hands trembled.

"You?" He stood still, his eyes fixed on a spot over her left shoulder.

"Yes." Her voice shook. "Claire and I can move in with Maisie and Ellie. They'll have us. You know they will."

He looked into her eyes, holding her gaze. He wasn't angry. He was assessing her.

"I'm sorry," he said. "I'm sorry, Cate. I'm just really exhausted."

Cate didn't know what to say. She hadn't expected an apology. "We need to talk," she repeated.

Allen went to the sofa and sat. "Do we have coffee?" He smiled. It was a tired, suffering smile. But a smile, nevertheless.

"Of course. I'll get you a cup." Relief weakened Cate's knees as she went into the kitchen. There—putting down her foot hadn't been so terrible after all. Deep down, under all the crusty layers, Allen loved her. That's why she'd married him. It'd be okay.

Cate poured a mug, waited until her hands stopped trembling, and carried it into the living room.

He took it without comment. Cate sat on the chair and waited.

When the mug was empty, Allen put it on the coffee table and looked at her. "You can't leave me, Cate. I need you."

Chapter 13

Cate held her breath. Allen wanted her to respond; she could see it in his eyes. "I don't want to leave either, Allen," she said finally, hearing the stress in her voice.

She needed to be frank. And she wasn't ready. She hadn't prepared.

Balancing on the edge of her chair, Cate pressed her knees together and smoothed her skirt. When she spoke, her voice wavered only a little. "I'm so tired of being snapped at. I'm trying to hold our marriage together, but I don't think I can do it any longer. Not without your help."

Again, Allen gazed over her shoulder. Cate saw his eyes going left, right, left, as if following a debate. Then he looked back. "Let's do it together then," he said. "We have to. For the girls. You want the girls to have both parents, don't you?"

Cate sat up straighter. "Of course I do." A stable family for Claire and Em was the number one priority. Two parents, enough money not to worry, house to live in or come back to, yard. The dream.

Only the marriage had become so toxic, staying in it wasn't a great example anymore. But if she and

Allen could work it out—that'd be best.

"I would like us to reconnect," Cate said, holding back some air in her lungs as if she were diving into water. "I would like us to tell each other how we feel. We haven't done that. We need to tell the truth from now on, Allen." It almost sounded like a warning, and so she blew out the last of her breath and made herself smile.

His Adam's apple moved. "Are you sure?" he asked. "What if you don't like the truth, Cate? How much do you want this?"

She grasped the edge of the chair. Her mouth was dry again. "Tell me everything, Allen."

"First I have to know you're on my side." He leaned toward her, bracing his elbows on his knees. "For us. For the girls. You can't make me talk and then use it against me."

"Of course not," Cate said, appalled. "Do you think I'd do something like that?"

He shook his head. "I need to hear you promise I'm safe. That this will bring us closer together, not farther apart."

Cate tilted her head. Allen sounded like he was setting up one of his trust exercises. Never once had she used a confidence against him. Allen was the one who did that to her. Maybe he hadn't noticed. "You're safe," she said. "I promise."

"Okay. Where are the kids?" He looked around as if he expected them to pop up from behind the sofa, the way they'd done when they were four years old.

"Claire's at a friend's. Em's working. She's got a

new job." Today was Em's first day at the Corner Café, though Allen didn't know about that.

Allen didn't ask. His chest expanded as he drew air. "Cate, I messed up."

Cate froze. Not fast. Slow. Ice crystalized in her chest one vein at a time, radiating outward the way frost spreads on a windshield in winter.

For years she'd wondered. "Who is she?"

His eyebrows rose. "Who is…" he repeated, and then he chuckled. "I don't have an *affair*, Cate," he said. "I can barely handle you."

Cate couldn't see the joke. What was funny?

The grin disappeared. "I'm serious. I don't have an affair," he repeated, actually reaching to touch her hand. "There's never been anyone else for me. How about you?"

"No," Cate said and wondered if she could pull her hand away.

There'd been so many pretty young assistants over the years; she'd almost been sure. Almost.

Was he lying?

Was she? About Calvin? Was Calvin her someone else?

"Of course not." Allen looked smug, as if Cate straying wasn't a possibility.

He didn't know she'd walked with Calvin, arms hooked tight, their attraction mutual. Even if she'd called it off in the end.

"What did you do?" Cate asked after a while. "What do you mean, you messed up?"

He frowned. "You know how hard it is for me to

get enough sleep."

"Yes, I do." Allen's insomnia had affected the household for years.

He pulled his hand away. Released, Cate rocked back into her chair.

"Well, it caught up with me." He paused.

Cate sat quietly. She didn't know what he meant.

"I had an accident last night," he continued. "I fell asleep at the wheel and drove into a store."

"Goodness!" Cate put a hand to her heart. "What happened? Are you okay?"

"I'm okay. I smashed the display window, but that's all. Thank you for caring."

"Of course."

"Now you know why I was quiet when I came in." He nodded. "I'm worried."

"What about? Tell me more. What happened, did you call the police, did they—"

"No." The word came hard and fast and firm. Final.

Cate looked up. "No? You didn't call the police? Why on earth not?"

He spread his hands as if it was obvious. "How can I call the cops, Cate? Think, for once."

Cate lowered her chin. "I don't see why you wouldn't, Allen."

"There'd be an official record of me falling asleep behind the wheel. Causing an accident because I was tired. Exhausted. Spent."

"It happens."

"Yes, but…" He broke off, and Cate felt the wave of his annoyance rise between them.

She had to keep him talking. "But?" she asked, gentle now.

"But duh," he said. "Can't you put one and one together? I've built a career getting insomniacs off their sleeping pills. How does it look if I fall asleep at the wheel? Can you even imagine having that bit of news plastered all over the media? My career would be over. Poof. No more money for the family. We need my income. Especially now, since you took a year off to stay home."

Cate pressed her lips together. "But how can you not report the accident, Allen? Was the window broken? How about the car?"

"Yes, yes, the window was smashed to bits. The car was fine; luckily, it was a rental with one of those rubber mats over the bumper. They didn't notice a thing when I returned it."

Cate was surprised at how much the rubber mat had helped. "You just drove away?"

"I left five hundred bucks cash to pay for the damage," Allen said. "Put it where they'd find it under a big shard. But yes, then I drove off."

"So you paid for the damage?"

He nodded. "It was a major chain. Not a mom-and-pop place barely holding on. A few calls will be made, a teen barista gets a day off and a local glazier will make some money."

"But?" Cate knew there'd be a *but*.

He shrugged his shoulders as if something was tickling his neck. "But I'm worried there was video surveillance. There always is these days, isn't there?"

Cate tucked her chin. "Could be." She tried to think. "What town was it? And what chain?"

He shook his head. "Better you don't know."

"Why's that better?"

Again he made a face as if she wasn't catching the obvious. "Because that way, they can't make you tell."

"Oh." Cate took a breath. "You think the cops might come looking for you?"

Allen stood and looked down on her. "Exactly. If they do come...will you tell them I was with you last night?"

Cate's heart drummed with stress, driving heat into her cheeks. She didn't want to lie to the police. "Is that wise, Allen? Don't they have your license plate on video?"

"I don't know. The license plate was splattered with mud. I was wearing a cap, so I don't think they got much of my face either."

"You don't think they can identify you?"

Allen came to stand by her chair and put a hand on her shoulder. It was almost shocking to Cate he would touch her like that—comforting, casual. Again she would've liked to shrug him off.

"They might suspect, but I don't think they can't tell for sure," he said. "Not if you say I was with you. No terrible damage was done to the store, Cate, but I could lose everything. Our marriage wouldn't survive, not with the stress it's already under. And you want our marriage to survive. Don't you? Don't you want to work for it?" He gripped her shoulder harder, tightening his hold.

Surely it was best to be upfront about the accident. Surely it was best to tell the cops the truth. Surely it was best not to lie and dodge and—

"I need your help," Allen said quietly. "Please, Cate. Stand by me. For our marriage. For our daughters. For love."

"Yes," Cate whispered. She'd wanted this, hadn't she? She'd wanted to know the truth, to connect, to be there for each other. She couldn't expect to start this new life with Allen handing her a bunch of flowers and a box of chocolates. "I'll stand by you. Will you stand by me?"

He squatted beside her chair. "Of course I will."

Cate thought that maybe he'd cradle her cheek in his hand the way he'd used to or even give her a kiss to seal their promise. But Allen only stared into her eyes for a moment. Then he rose and went into the kitchen.

Cate could hear him pour a glass of water. He drank, the sound of his swallows slow and methodical.

Chapter 14

It was a Fish Market day. Ellie flipped the sign in the door from Closed to Open, then went into the backroom, washed her hands and pulled a bowl with fresh herring from the fridge. She readied her cutting board and slapped a fish on it.

The filleting knife was nice and sharp. Ellie picked it up, studied the edge, then raised it—and set it back down. "Ugh."

The fish was staring at her, eye glazed white. "Ugh, ugh," Ellie whispered again.

She didn't want to cut into the silvery skin. She wanted the herring to be alive, swimming in the ocean in a school of its own. Eyes clear. Looking for predators and plankton and pretty herring ladies.

Ellie pressed the heels of her palms against her temples.

It was getting worse. She'd never had a problem filleting fish before. Now it bothered her all the time.

Working only every other day at the store wasn't helpful; it threw off her rhythm. She'd started doing it a few weeks ago, rearranging her schedule so she'd have time to help with the inn.

It was enjoyable picking out bed sheets and furniture. It was entertaining to fight with Maisie about color schemes. It was exciting trying out recipes.

Cutting up fish, once an art form to her, wasn't any of these things anymore. Something had changed.

Ellie cast her mind back, trying to remember when it had started.

Months ago, Bonnie had sold her three lobsters. Two were dusky red, one a shimmering green. Two garnets. One emerald.

Dale was determined to eat them, so Ellie released them back into the sea. They deserved it. And that had been the beginning.

Ever since, she'd wanted to set every sea creature free. Bonnie kept bringing her spectacular specimens; queens and kings of the sea. Much too precious to die. Definitely too pretty to eat.

The deliveries had stopped after Bonnie's thing with Dale had come out, but Ellie remembered every single clam, all the fish, each mussel.

Yet she hadn't rescued a single one. Instead, she'd sold them. After all, she was a fishmonger, and that's how she earned her money.

Tried to, anyway.

Ellie slipped the herring back in the bowl, carried it to the display and quickly arranged the uncut fish on ice. Whoever bought them could slice them up themselves.

Afterward she stood, drumming her fingers on the steel counter and staring out the window.

Mid-September sometimes brought rain, and rain washed away the last tourists. The season was almost over. There wouldn't be many people buying fish to grill at the beach anymore.

Little Madame Botrel would still make bouillabaisse for her son's family. A small handful of other locals frequented the Fish Market too. Vince bought mussels sometimes. Or shrimp. But most people bought their seafood at the supermarket or caught what they needed.

The door opened with a slurping sound, and startled, Ellie looked up. "Oh." She straightened from her easy slouch and pursed her lips. "It's *you*."

"It's me," Gordy confirmed and pulled the knit seaman's cap off his mob of black hair. "Hi, Ellie."

Ellie crossed her arms.

Gordy was one of the local fishermen. In the summer, when tourists fell on Beach Cove like wealthy locusts, the man put a food truck on the parking lot by the seawall. During the day, he cooked his catch; lobster rolls, blackened fish, fried calamari, fish and chips. His prices were exorbitant. Ridiculous. But even Ellie had to admit his food was delicious; she'd seen grown men fight over Gordy's last beer-battered bass. The Starfish Report had published an article about the incident.

Gordy was also one of those fishermen who'd never sold Ellie a single fish.

Not even when she'd first started out. She'd been trying hard to woo the local suppliers back then. But because her family hadn't lived for centuries in

Beach Cove like his own, Gordy had branded her a greenhorn, come to exploit the community.

It had put the other fishers off. They'd never straight-up said it, but many didn't sell Ellie their wares either. No, the catch had to go to the big market in Bay Port, sorry. Better prices and old connections and all that. You know.

Ellie knew. She knew Gordy had egged them on.

In fact, he could well be blamed for the fact that her store had never thrived. Instead, it had turned into a thorn in the flesh of her marriage.

"What can I do for you?" she asked now, feeling as warm and fuzzy as the chipped ice in the display case.

"Always so angry." Gordy planted himself in front of the counter and crossed his arms, too.

"I'm not," she declared frostily. "What do you want?"

"I want to know why you talk like that," he said. "Am I the only one you talk to like that?"

"Like what."

"Like *that*."

"That's how I talk. What can I get you? Herring's on sale."

"Is that all you've got?" He squinted at the glass. "Don't you at least filet them?"

Ellie didn't deign to answer. "Do you want to buy herring or not, Gordy?"

He shook his head. "Why can't you give me one straight answer, Ellie?"

If she were young and energetic, Ellie would've rolled her eyes. But she was too old. "Why don't you answer mine? Do you want a herring, yes or no?"

"No, I don't want your herring. They're tiny, all skin and bones."

"Oh well, then there's the door behind you." Ellie pointed. Not only did he not mean to buy anything, he was insulting her fish. It was just like him.

"Wait a moment. Wait." Gordy frowned at the floor. Then he looked up at the ceiling. "I'll take one herring."

"Too late." Ellie shifted her weight to the other foot. "You can't have one."

"But I want one!" Gordy's face started to flush.

Ellie watched with interest. "You need to eat more vegetables, Gordy," she commented. "Less red meat. You're the apoplectic type."

Gordy ran a hand through his hair, pulling the ends. "I'm not apoplectic. I want to buy a herring."

"No, it's too late. Next customer, please."

"There aren't any," Gordy said, checking over his shoulder. "Why are you so mean to me?"

Something like pity almost pooled in Ellie's stomach. But not really. He'd been much meaner to her. "Because I can."

"Makes no sense!" Gordy flushed even deeper, but he still didn't turn to leave. "Makes no sense you're mean to me, Ellie. You're nice to everyone else."

Ellie leaned forward. "We're not playing recess at middle school, Gordon. Why do you keep coming to my store? I don't like you. You made my life hard when I first started, and I don't like you for it. I'm not mean; I barely scratch your feelings with my words.

You were mean. My store never was a success because you spread word I was an outsider who didn't deserve the support of my community." She gasped for breath. *Now* she was angry. "My business never recovered from you. Get out. I don't want to talk shop with you. Find someone else."

Gordy stared. Ellie started to pull the herring back into the bowl. If he wasn't going to leave, she was. There'd be no sales today anyway, and if she went home, at least she and Maisie could try out the new bread recipes. Ellie would drop off the herring at Maison de Sand on her way home. Madame would gladly turn it into soup for her daughter-in-law.

"What are you doing?" Gordy asked after a moment.

"I'm closing." Ellie covered the bowl with plastic wrap and started to scoop the ice into the sink. A quick rinse, a flip of the sign in the door, and she'd be outta here.

"Because of me?" Gordy scratched his beard. "Because of things I might've said or done almost thirty years ago?"

Scoop mid-air, Ellie glared at him. "Thirty years of consequences to deal with, Gordy. My life would be totally different if you hadn't been so hard on me when I opened the store. Now look at it!" She felt like tossing the dead fish at his head. "Business is so bad I don't even want to do it anymore! Not to mention my marriage broke up over it!"

"That can't be true," Gordy said quietly. "Come on."

She shrugged him off. "It's true."

It wasn't true. Or maybe it was. Who knew? If she'd have worked out a deal with the local fishermen when she was getting established, if she'd have gotten better ware cheaper—who knew how she'd have done? If life would've been easier, maybe she and Dale could've made it.

Uh, no. Dale was rotten. And love couldn't be bought, nor the goodwill that made a marriage successful. She wasn't about to admit it to Gordy, though, since it was none of his business. He deserved to feel bad.

"I heard your marriage broke up because of Bonnie Sagartati," Gordy said and pushed his hands into the pockets of his jeans. Ellie glared. He stood in front of her counter as if he were on a ship in the rolling sea. Legs apart, knees unlocked to counter the waves crashing into the keep.

"It's nothing to do with—" Ellie tossed the last ice in the sink. Did everyone in town know about Dale's infidelity?

The girls hadn't talked; Ellie was sure of it. But Beach Cove was a small town. Everyone knew everyone else, and a pair of eager ears a table over was enough to pick up a hushed discussion.

"Get out, Gordy. No more fish. The store's closed."

He unraveled his arms and held up his hands, showing his palms as if he were a bringer of peace. "Hold on, firecracker. It's not my fault people talk. I *always* thought Dale was a douche."

"Yes, well, thanks for letting me know. It's not

helpful." It wasn't. She'd figured it out on her own, and she didn't need anyone, least of all Gordy, to rub it in.

"Your kid's great, though," Gordy said. "Nice restaurant. He's doing real good."

"Stop it." Ellie knew what he was doing. Her son was her soft spot. Already, the flattery found the target, and her heart softened. Tommy *was* doing good. Gordy admitting it meant the old families had welcomed him with open arms. Even once the last tourist left, local patrons would keep his business running.

She put her hands on the counter. "What are you really doing here, Gordy? What do you want from me?"

They were about the same age, but unlike her, the years had done him good. The silver woven through his beard made him look less like a sasquatch. His body, pitted each day against the sea herself, was hard with muscle; lean but powerful.

There wasn't a ship in the harbor Gordy couldn't work, Ellie thought. He could steer any vessel past the bluffs into the open Atlantic. He knew where the underwater cliffs were, the schedule of ebb and tide, the habits of sea creatures.

"What do you want from me?" she repeated, her voice no longer harsh. Her temper flared easily. Just as quickly, it settled again.

"Nothing." He looked down at the cap on his hands. "Maybe..." He cleared his throat. "Maybe I'm sorry for...all that." He gestured at the empty display, awkward like a teenager.

An apology? Ellie tilted her head. Twenty-something years ago, Gordy had been a different man. Young, and so arrogant. The self-proclaimed leader of the locals, the defender of Beach Cove's ancestral spirit as he saw it.

She'd been a different person too. Naive and idealistic, in love with a vapid man and business plans she'd based on nothing. Turned out she'd been wrong too, building her life on shifting sand.

They'd all changed. All of them. Ellie had no trouble accepting it for herself and her friends. Why not extend the courtesy to Gordy? He was doing his best to scrape a living off the sea. It wasn't easy.

Now he stood in her store, listening and apologizing. Life had humbled his arrogance. Ellie had had a taste of it herself. If she'd be living in the store attic instead of running Beach Cove Inn, she'd not be so brash with Gordy either.

"Okay," she said softly. She'd think about forgiving him. "Thanks, Gordy."

For a moment there was silence between them. Gordy's eyes were an exceptionally light blue; the color of water washing over sand. They were too light for his weathered skin.

"I just wanted to check if you had any shrimp," Gordy finally said. His chest heaved as if he wanted to say something else, but then he only pulled his cap back on and nodded. "See you around, Ellie." He crossed the store, pulled the door open and left.

The door shut with a quiet slurp.

"Yeah," Ellie murmured into the silence, watching

the fisherman stride away with long legs and stiff knees. "See you around, Gordy."

She went to the door, watching until he turned the corner and she couldn't see him anymore. Then she shook her head, turned the lock and flipped the sign.

Chapter 15

Cate pulled back the curtain of the bedroom window. She was still wet from the shower, barefoot, clutching a towel around herself.

She'd heard a car. A blue Ford had parked in the driveway.

Two officers inside, talking and glancing at the house. Pointing at papers on the dash, flipping pages.

Cate dropped the curtain and tiptoed back into the bathroom. Lucky she'd laid out her clothes the night before. Hastily, she slipped them on. When she buttoned her blouse, her hands shook enough to make it difficult.

They'd come. She had to lie for Allen and her marriage.

She zipped the good skirt—not too long, not too short—checking her reflection in the mirror. Her face was pale and distorted by condensation running down the glass. Foggy like a ghost.

This wasn't her. None of this was her.

Cate braced her hands on the sink and inhaled.

She wanted more honesty in her marriage. She wanted Allen to tell her the truth. Nobody had said it was easy. Life wasn't a fairytale.

An image of Helene's face flashed through her mind. What would she say if she knew Cate was getting ready to lie to the police?

The doorbell rang, the sound quick and hard like a striking hand.

"Cate?" Allen's voice came from downstairs. "Could you get that, honey?"

A shiver crawled down her spine. He was performing for the cops. They'd be on the welcome mat, waiting, listening at the door.

"Yes, Allen. I'm coming." Cate grabbed the hairbrush and tugged it through her short gray strands. She could do it. It wasn't like he'd committed a crime. A chain franchise had a damaged window. A quick job for the local glazier. Nothing more.

She hurried downstairs and opened the door.

Outside stood two officers in uniform; a man and a woman. "Are you Mrs. Clark, ma'am?"

"Yes?" She didn't know which one had asked. And where was Allen? Wasn't he going to come to the door, too?

"We have a few questions. Do you have a minute?"

Cate rubbed her chin to hide the pulse beating in her neck. "Of course. Come in. This is about a former student?" She'd thought of that before, the former student.

There'd been one once, suspected of setting fire to a hay barn in Sandville. The police had asked if she knew where he was.

In the end, they'd found him at home with his

parents. No smoke in his hair, no burns on his hands, no dirt on his sneakers. Not as much as a match in his car. It ended up being someone else.

Cate remembered how it'd felt to talk to the officer. She'd thought his suspicion was absurd. The student had been a sweet kid, punctual and polite, whose only fault turned out to be a first name shared with the offender. Cate groped for that headspace again, but she was too nervous.

She gestured tightly at the sofa, wondering where Allen had gone. Was he listening?

The cops sat, hands on knees, and introduced themselves with ranks and names. Cate could barely make sense of the syllables, let alone remember them. "Can I get you coffee?" She ran a shaky hand through her hair. It was wet. She stared at it. "I'm sorry, I'm straight out of the shower."

"No worries," the man—Willis? Wallis?—said. "No need for coffee either. May we ask you a few quick questions, Mrs. Clark? Why don't you sit? I feel like I should be standing myself."

Cate obeyed, picking the armchair. Why didn't Allen come and lie for himself when she had to? "Okay," she said. "How can I help you?"

"Just a routine check, going over a couple of things." The man smiled. "You're married to Allen Clark?"

Cate couldn't breathe. "Going on twenty years. *Thirty*, I mean. Thirty years."

"Yes..." The female cop was flipping through papers on a clipboard. Cate couldn't see what was written on them. "And he lives here?"

"Yes," Cate said. "Uh, what's this about? I thought it was about a student?"

"Just routine," the woman said. She looked tired.

"Are you sure you don't want coffee? It's no trouble." Despite her anxiety, Cate wanted the woman to look less tired. She shouldn't be sent to question people, looking this exhausted. She should be at home.

"No, thanks." The woman gave Cate a brief smile. "I've had too much already. Would you mind telling us what it is your husband does?"

"Like, for work?" Cate was surprised. What did that have to do with the crashed window? "He runs seminars."

"What kind of seminars?"

"He teaches meditation and relaxation techniques. Trust exercises to bring corporate employees closer." Cate tried to think. "It makes for a better work environment," she added.

Allen used to tell her about the seminars. It'd been repetitive, with Allen always complaining about the same things. She'd become bored of the stories before Allen stopped telling them.

"I don't know much about his work," she now explained, feeling like she had to give them more. "I'm a teacher and have kids. I don't have time to go with him."

"Have you been to his seminars?" The man shifted the heavy belt on his waist so he could lean back. "How are they?"

"I've been to a few before we had the girls."

Cate paused. She felt like she'd been to some since then, but... "Honestly," she said, hearing how unsure she sounded, "either I just can't remember, or I haven't gone in a while." She laughed, embarrassed. "Goodness. Well, like I said. Going on thirty years now."

The woman nodded reassuringly, but Cate saw her glance at her partner. "Was Mr. Clark at one of his seminars last week? Or was he at home?"

Cate sat back and folded her hands on her lap. Here it was. "Yes," she said. Then she cleared her throat. "Yes," she repeated, louder this time so Allen could hear her say it. Wherever he was.

"Yes? Which one?"

"At home." Cate caught herself shaking her head and stopped. "He was here the entire week. At home."

"He never left?" The woman blinked. "Not even once?"

"Oh well, I guess he did go to the store and things like that. He was just—generally home." Cate felt like her stomach was liquefying. How much was too much to say? What was too little?

"Where did he go? I mean, on those short trips away from the house."

Cate's brain stuttered as if the cop had stuck twigs in its gears. "I don't know," she said, helpless. "Maybe he went to get bagels or fill up the car? I don't usually —" She cast around for words, ideas, anything. "I don't always pay attention."

"But you think he might've gone to get bagels?" The man pulled a pencil out of his breast pocket and handed it to his partner.

"I don't know," Cate said. "Maybe?"

"So you don't know."

"Um. Not really." Cate inhaled a flat breath which lodged in her chest and made her cough. If Allen was listening, he'd be angry. She wasn't doing it right. It wasn't good enough. She had to try harder.

"But that's...*normal*." Cate stumbled over the first words, tried to catch herself with the last. "I do know he's been home. He slept mostly. He's always tired because he works so much, and he catches up on sleep when he's here. Yes. I don't think he went to get bagels after all. Or gas."

The female officer nodded. "Is there anybody else in the house?"

"My daughter lives here." Cate went to the bookshelf and picked up a framed photo of Claire. Glad to have something to hold on to, she brought it to the sofa like some sort of evidence. "But she's busy with sports and friends."

The man leaned forward, ignoring the photo. "What about Allen's colleagues? Do you know them? Can you give us names?"

Cate put the photo on the side table, buying time by adjusting the support at the back of the frame. The question made no sense to her. The officer sounded so sure Allen *had* colleagues.

She looked up. "Allen works alone. He only has mentees who help with the events."

"Do you know their names?"

"No." Cate wondered if she should tell them the

mentees were usually young women with skinny waists and pretty faces. Except for last week, when it'd been a young man with hard eyes and a hood.

The officers sat for a moment longer. Suddenly, they stood as if a secret alarm had rung. Cate rose as well.

"Thank you," the woman said. Her voice was sad. "Can we come back if we have more questions?"

Cate nodded, though it was the last thing she wanted. She walked them to the entrance, and when they stepped outside, she did too. She closed the door, so Allen couldn't hear.

"What's this about?" she whispered. "Can you please tell me?"

They looked at her. "Is your husband home now?" the man asked.

"I don't know," Cate whispered. "I just don't know."

Chapter 16

Ellie laid her fork on the kitchen table.

"You don't like it?" Tom grabbed the fork and prodded the cherry chocolate cake as if he were a surgeon.

"I do like it," Ellie said. "I just don't have an appetite."

Her son scooped up both crumb and cream and chewed thoughtfully. "But it's good." He speared a luscious Amarena cherry. "*Really* good."

"I know it is. It's not the cake. I'm worried."

"Yeah?" He stopped eating. "Why?"

They were sitting in the corner kitchen of his apartment, overlooking the marketplace. The sun was just starting to topple off its azure peak, and across the square, the Corner Café was buzzing. Not with tourists, but with Beach Cove's very own lunch crowd.

Ellie squinted to make out the patrons sitting at the bistro tables outside. Fishermen and their wives indulged in tea and torte, Madame's daughter-in-law ate strudel and read a book, the harbor master and his son, laughing, shared pizza, no salad. Gordy hadn't lied. The community supported Tom; he'd be okay.

More than that. He'd be great.

"Hey Mom? What are you worried about?"

"I don't know," Ellie said, returning her attention to her son. She smiled, letting him know it was fine. "Maybe I'm anxious because…" Ellie thought. "Our first guest arrives soon."

"Your inn is ready for guests. You were ready months ago."

"I know. It's all nerves. We want to make a good first impression."

"What else?"

"Cate's been out of touch." She shrugged. "Allen's come back."

"Maybe she needs a bit of peace and quiet after staying with you and Maisie?"

"Funny." Ellie threw him a look. "She's not answering her phone. We can see she's reading texts, but she's not texting back."

"Why don't you stop by her place and check in?" Tom picked up the plate and carried it to the sink, then returned with a cup of tea. He set it before Ellie. "I can ask Em to do it if you want."

Ellie inhaled the tea's smoky fragrance. "How is Em doing, working at the Café?"

"Oh, great. So far she's doing great." Tom sat back down, but there was a restless look in his eyes.

"She's a good baker, isn't she? She's helped Maisie come up with a peach upside-down cake that blew us away."

"I should try it."

"So she mostly bakes?" Ellie raised an eyebrow.

"What's going on? Cat's got your tongue?"

"No. Yes." He looked at the ceiling. "She's great."

"But? How much cake are you selling?"

"A ton." Tom put his elbows on the table. "Em's only just started, Mom. She *is* doing great, but she's so... I don't know if she's going to stick around. Yesterday, she wanted to be a teacher. The day before that, she wanted to be a surgeon."

"I think she was too traumatized by Alex's disappearance for med school. She said it was too hard to see cadavers and body parts while worrying about her best friend. I don't blame her for not following through."

"What if she doesn't know what she wants?"

Ellie looked up, surprised. "Then she leaves to find out. You can find someone else, no?"

He spread his hands. "Like who? There's no one else!"

"That can't be true." There were lots of talented young people in Beach Cove. Weren't there? "What about Becky? She won a prize for her blueberry cobbler at the fair. Remember?"

"Becky Jonas?" Tom dropped his chin. "She was nine years old when she won that prize."

"So she'll be even better now."

"I bet it was her mom making the cobbler. Or her nana. Nana Jonas died years ago."

"Oookay." Ellie drummed her fingers on the table. She'd meant to only stay a minute because Maisie wanted her at the inn to go over menus. Then again, they already had about five years' worth of breakfast and dinner options, cross-referenced alphabetically on a spreadsheet.

They could wing the menu.

More importantly, something in Tommy's voice set her maternal alarm ringing. Ellie stopped drumming. "Are you going to ask Becky or not?" she demanded. "Just to see if she's interested."

He glanced at the ceiling. "She's married."

"What does that have to do with anything? Do you need your bakers to be single?"

"It means she'll be busy with her family, and probably she's got a job already, and— Look Mom, I don't even know if Becky Jonas lives in Beach Cove anymore. Last I talked with her, we were both in elementary school."

"You don't like Becky?"

He sighed. "I like Em."

"Of course you do." Tom, Alex and Em had always been made to play with each other. Lucky for her, Maisie and Cate, the kids had gotten along well. They'd hung out daily even after the maternally prescribed playdates had ended.

Siblings, practically.

Ellie eyed Tom.

He returned her gaze helplessly. "I need her to stay, Mom. She's got half a foot out the door. I can tell. If I can't keep her, she'll leave Beach Cove."

Ellie leaned forward. "She's never really gotten over Alex," she said gently. "Maybe she *needs* to get out of Beach Cove."

"No, she needs to stay," Tommy repeated. "She's

been to Boston. It didn't do her any good. She was different when she came back. On edge. Depressed. She's my best friend, Mom. I can't stand it when she's unhappy."

"Well... I think it's because she and Allen butted heads when she came back. He gave her grief for dropping out. Of course, there was a lot of money gone down the drain too. It wasn't easy for Cate and Allen to help with the tuition—and then nothing came of it."

"Living in a house with Allen hasn't helped." Tom's brows drew together as if he'd like a word with Allen. "Luckily, she got out of there."

Ellie's thoughts flew back to Cate. Em had moved out, and Allen was back. Ellie felt her forehead crumble. "I wished Cate would get a divorce," she said darkly. "It's been getting worse."

"Cate doesn't mind?"

"Oh, she minds," Ellie said. "It's hard to tell why she doesn't leave, but you never know unless you're in the relationship yourself. I've got a feeling she's scared of Allen. She's never admitted it, though."

Tom clenched a fist. Ellie took it into her own hands. "Em's all right. She's out of the house. I guess Claire's going to stay with her a lot?"

He nodded. "Claire's sleeping on the futon couch. At the moment, it's only Cate and Allen at the house."

"She's got her sister visiting, too."

Tom looked like he wanted to say something but then let it go. He pulled his hand back. "So give me your seasoned advice, Mom. How do I keep Em in Beach Cove?"

"I don't know," Ellie said. "Emily's entire life is here. Her family, her job, a brand-new apartment. What else does she need?"

He shifted his chair, discontent. "I'd like her to have a proper job," he said finally. "You know, not just work for me, but build something she'll be proud of."

"Are you proud of the Corner Café, Tommy?"

He stood. "I am. I'm proud of the food and how much people like it, and I'm proud to provide jobs. I can't imagine throwing it away and taking off. Besides, I love Beach Cove."

"Beach Cove loves you back," Ellie said and pointed at the window. "Look. People value what you've given the town."

Chapter 17

Tom braced his hands on the windowsill, gazing out at his restaurant. Then he straightened. "A bakery," he declared.

"What?" Ellie thought she'd missed the beginning of the sentence.

Her son turned to her. "A bakery. I can open a bakery with Em."

When the words sank in, Ellie's first instinct was to hold her breath. Then she blew it out, slow and quiet, so as not to hurt any feelings. "You mean, open a bakery in Beach Cove? With Em, who you think is already halfway out the door?"

"Yes!" He plopped into his chair and ran his hands through his hair. "That's what I mean." His gaze turned inward. "I think it could work."

"Uh..."

But he interrupted her. "Listen, Mom. The Corner Café was meant to be a restaurant. That's where I cook. All that cake business is really too much for the space. We make do, but it's a logistical nightmare. We can't bake nearly enough. And I don't like telling people they can't have cake because it's pizza time." He thought for a moment. "You'd be surprised how mad people can get when they want cake and can't have any."

"I've come across it." Just the day before, Kenny and Steve Cobb, two fishers as red-faced and hard-shelled as any lobster the cove had produced, had cornered Ellie in the supermarket. They'd complained bitterly about missing out on Tommy's raspberry roll because their dinghy's engine had failed. When they'd finally made it ashore, all the cream tortes had been eaten and crossed off the menu.

Her son nodded, satisfied. "I'm going to crunch some numbers," he said. "And then I'm going to ask Emily if she wants in."

Ellie bit her tongue. Seemed like a bad idea to start a business with a girl with wanderlust, but it was her son's life. His decision. "And if she does," she said when she could, "where are you going to put her?"

"I don't know." Tommy rubbed his chin. "Not too many places in Beach Cove I can rent. Maybe if I build myself?"

Ellie leaned forward. "Tommy, you're one successful season from going broke. I know it's going well, but you're just starting. You don't have money to *build*, do you?"

He dropped his hand and sighed. "No. I don't."

"Besides, you're not allowed to build near the village or coast. You'd be too far away for foot traffic."

"I hadn't thought of that. We do need to be in the village to make it work."

Ellie stood and walked to the stove where she

inspected the shiny cooktop, then went to the open window. The frame was cracked, and she pried off a speck of paint. Catty-corner, the Café was fuller than before; a family circled the tables like a flock of hungry gulls. When they couldn't find an empty spot, they walked away.

Ellie flicked the paint outside. She too felt the need to move. She wanted to bake bread and thin out the Japanese anemones with Maisie, and she still had to go buy cream for their guest.

Already, word had gotten out that Beach Cove Inn had opened its doors. Maisie's inbox exploded with questions about rooms and dates, things to do and dietary requests. The inn could easily book out for the winter. Already Maisie was talking about a hot tub overlooking the frozen cove, cross-country skiing, writing retreats.

Despite their slow start, Ellie knew the inn would do well. *Very* well.

Then she thought of the beautiful, dead sea creatures she laid out on ice. She thought of Madame stirring her bouillabaisse while her daughter-in-law ate alone at the Corner Café.

Ellie turned to her son. "Use the Fish Market," she said. "You'll have to remodel the kitchen, take out the freezers and put in ovens. It's not going to be a big bakery. But it'll serve Beach Cove."

Tommy's eyes widened. "The Market is your store. You can't give it up. You love fish."

She smiled. "I love fish alive. Selling dead ones has become an ordeal. Strange, huh?"

It took a moment for him to speak. "You don't have to do this for me, Mom. I'll find another solution."

She patted his shoulder. "I'm serious about the fish. It's been happening slowly ever since I released Bonnie's lobsters back into the sea."

"You did? How many?"

Ellie smiled. "Three, the magical number. It was beautiful."

"I didn't know. Why didn't you tell me about this?"

"Honestly, I didn't think it mattered, and we both had enough to deal with."

"So what changed?" Tom asked, his eyes not leaving her face. Ellie could tell he was watching for signs that giving up the store was a sacrifice, not the relief she claimed.

"Everything, kid." She went around the table; there was nowhere left to go, so she sat back down. "The inn, mainly. We can host more guests if I fully commit, and it'll be much more lucrative than the store. Besides, I'm glad to get out. The Market only reminds me of the past."

"You mean Dad." His jaw hardened. Tom was angry at Dale for abandoning them.

Ellie hummed a yes. The market had always stood between her and her ex-husband. In the end, Dale had used the store to blame the divorce on Ellie.

"I'm starting something new," she said. "I love our inn, and I enjoy working with Maisie."

Tom stood, ran his hands through his hair, sat again. "I'd be more than happy to take the building off your hands if you're sure. Not for free, of course. I'll pay the market price."

Ellie wanted to protest, then remembered how little Dale had paid for the store. It'd make Tom happy to properly own the building and feel like he was taking care of her. She could use the money to start a college fund for Tommy's future kids.

"Okay," she said. "You pay over the next ten years what your father paid. It's all yours."

His forehead smoothed, and his shoulders relaxed. Ellie stood, too joyous to stay seated. This was good. Very good. "It's going to be great," she said. "It feels right. Sam always says to follow our intuition, and mine says well done."

"Thank you, Mom," Tom said. "I promise I'll make it work for us."

"And Em," Ellie said. "Make it work for Emily, too."

He didn't reply, but his determination filled the space between them.

Ellie lifted her purse off the back of the chair and fussed with the strap on her shoulder, pretending to be busier than she was to give Tom a moment. Her son was in love. It was possible he'd been in love with Cate's daughter since they went to school together.

Ellie tried to keep a check on her smile.

It explained why he'd never dated anyone. It used to worry her. But if he'd been in love with Em all this time, it made sense. "Bye, Tommy," she said finally. "I'll get the deed ready. And I'd love to see a proper business plan for the bakery."

He looked like a rock. Still and unmoving, hands

flat on the table, eyes unfocused, smile too fixed.

Ellie swallowed a laugh. He'd had the same look on his face the year he'd gotten the Vespa for Christmas. This was how her son looked trying to keep it together. Petrified by joy.

"Bye," she said again, then went and pressed a kiss on his head. To her surprise he jumped up, chair screeching over the floor, reaching with long arms to pull her into a bear hug.

"Best mom ever," he said. "You're great."

"Oh, well. Hardly." Ellie patted his back, and now she really did have to laugh.

Chapter 18

Tires crunched in the driveway gravel.

Maisie slapped Ellie's arm. "That's him!"

"Sheesh, I know. Obviously." Ellie rubbed her arm.

Maisie cleared her throat. "Sorry, Ells. I didn't mean to do that. I got carried away."

"Let's stay calm. We've got this."

Yes indeed. Though it was also the beginning of a new era. Maisie straightened her shoulders and held her breath for a count of eight.

It'd be great.

She knew how to host. Robert used to invite tons of guests and business partners to Beach House. Plus, she and Ellie were prepared: they had lemon tarts and pear cobbler for tea, Italian wedding soup, stuffed mushrooms and chicken skewers for dinner. There were Portuguese linens on the beds, Turkish robes in the bathrooms, and the correct color curtains on the windows.

The rest was all about being gracious. Hospitable and talkative. But also not get on the man's last nerve.

Outside, a car door slammed shut. A moment later, the deeper thud of a closing trunk, and then tires pulling back on the road.

Maisie and Ellie stood in the entrance hall, waiting for the doorbell.

There it was.

"You open it," Ellie whispered. "Where do I go? Quick, tell me!"

Maisie looked at her, surprised. Here she'd thought she was the nervous one. "I don't know—in the kitchen?"

"The kitchen? I don't want to be in the—"

But Maisie had already left her side, striding to the door. With every step, she sank more into herself, becoming cool and collected. Ellie's nerves had calmed her own.

The bell chimed a second time, and she opened the door.

"Hello." A man in his late fifties or early sixties stood on the bottom stair, smiling. He held a sleek black suitcase in his hand. "I assume this is the Beach Cove Inn?" he asked in a British accent and nodded at the brass sign.

"Yes, it is." Maisie smiled back. "You must be William Glace."

"So I am. And you are Mrs. Jameson?"

"That's me. Please, come in." Maisie stepped aside to let her visitor in.

William at once reminded her of Vince, even though William was a little smaller and a lot rounder, with dark cocoa eyes. But he too wore a button-down shirt with rolled sleeves, slacks, no jacket, and there was something about the way he moved that was familiar.

He walked in, and Maisie closed the door. William set his suitcase on the floor and brought his hands together in a silent clap. "I understand I'm the first guest," he said. "At least Vincent said so. What an honor! The house is exceptionally beautiful. I was crossing my fingers the car would stop and not drive past."

The little flattery did the trick; Maisie saw Ellie beam at William and knew she was doing the same.

"I'm Ellie, nice to meet you," Ellie said. "Are you from England?"

"I'm afraid I very much am." The man lowered his head in what amounted to a little bow. "Did Vincent tell on me?"

"Do you know him from London?" Maisie joined in. "Isn't that where Vince is from?"

"No, nothing so urban," Will said vaguely. "I'm from up north, from a small, rather unknown village in the Dales." He bent to again pick up his suitcase.

Maisie thought she detected another similarity to Vince—an unwillingness to answer questions. Why not say the name of his small, rather unknown village in the Dales? He also hadn't confirmed that Vince was a Londoner. Surely, he'd know if he was as good a friend as Vince claimed.

"Would you like to see your room?" She gestured the way. "And then maybe a quick tour of the house? Or you can settle in and take your time; the flight must've been exhausting. We're here if you need anything."

"A tour would be nice, thank you very much indeed." William's dark eyes scanned Maisie as if she were a barcode, full of hidden information to decipher.

"Great! Let's get that luggage taken care of." Ellie still seemed nervously excited, waving their guest. "This way to your room, please."

"Here's the key," Maisie said and pressed the key —not a card, but a proper key with a beard—into William's hand. "Should I let Vince know you've arrived?"

Something twinkled in the man's eye. Maisie wondered if she'd unintentionally said something funny.

"Vincent...uh, Vince already knows. But thank you for offering. How very kind of you." He followed Ellie, who led the way.

Maisie stayed where she was, looking after them.

Before he disappeared into the kitchen, William looked back over his shoulder. "I called Vincent when I landed in Boston," he explained. "He said he'd meet me here if that's all right. By the way, please call me Will."

"I'm Maisie," Maisie replied.

Ellie and Will left, exchanging pleasantries about the weather. Maisie went into the kitchen and tied on an apron.

The tray of lemon tarts was cooling by the window, but now she wanted to make something else too. Baking, she'd found, was good for the soul. The rhythmic kneading of dough, the gentle sifting of flour, the energetic beating of butter and sugar and eggs felt therapeutic.

Maisie decided on Franzbroetchen, light and doughy rolls brimming with cinnamon sugar. She and Robert used to have them in northern Germany, where the skies were weepy and the bakeries full of hot coffee and sweet treats.

She was warming butter and milk on the stove when Ellie returned.

"Smells good." Ellie peeped into the pot. "What are you making?"

"Franzbroetchen." Maisie did her best to pronounce the throaty r and sharp z, the loopy, drunken 'oe' sound. As usual, her attempt failed. "Did you notice he didn't tell us where he's from? Just somewhere in the Dales."

Ellie squinted. "I don't know where the Dales are, let alone any towns in the Dales. Do you?"

The butter was almost melted. Maisie measured and poured sugar into the pot. "You think that's why?"

"Yes, I think that's why." Ellie went to the fridge and took out the pitcher of lemonade. The ice chinked invitingly. "He's going to take a few minutes to freshen up and unpack. I got the feeling it wasn't a great flight."

"It's terribly long." Maisie didn't enjoy airplanes, not even flying first class. The air smelled of plastic and chemicals, and she always felt a little nauseated breathing it.

"You think he likes lemonade?" Ellie put the pitcher on the counter.

"I don't know, Ellie. You think he'd give us a

straight answer if we asked?"

"Of course he would, you're too suspicious. Hey, I have to tell you about Tom," Ellie said. "And we should probably go check on Cate, make sure she's okay."

The doorbell chimed for a third time, and they both looked up.

Chapter 19

Ellie went to answer the door, leaving Maisie to wonder about Tom and Cate. A few moments later, Ellie reappeared. Walking behind her, shoulders stooped and eyes lidded, was Vince.

"Hi," Maisie greeted him. It was good to see her neighbor, even in his hidden version. "Your friend arrived only a moment ago."

"How are you, Maisie?" He came closer to where she stood at the stove. Close enough she thought she could sense the warmth of his body.

"Very well. Mixing sugar and butter." She tilted the pot to show her foamy proof.

"It already looks delicious." For a brief moment, Vince's irises came out of hiding and were warm and gray like summer rain. "I'm stopping by to say hello to William."

"Will, he said to call him," Ellie threw in. Her eyes were flicking from Vince to Maisie and back.

"I bet he did." Vince raised an eyebrow. "I suppose it's fair to warn you William's generally well-behaved, but he'll try to worm his way into your good graces. I don't at all think he's good enough for either one of

141

you. You're much too lovely for him."

Maisie snorted, but Ellie clapped her hands. "We'll only ever have British guests, Maisie," she said happily. "They're so *cute*."

"Quite." Vince looked so pleased, even Maisie had to laugh. "Well, if you'll excuse me," he said. "I'd much rather stay and chat with you, but since I said I would, I should go greet…*Will*."

"Leaves stage left," Maisie remarked when the echo of his steps had gone. "He's laying it on a bit thick, isn't he?"

Ellie stabbed a knowing finger into the air. "He's jealous, Maisie. You know he is."

"Nonsense." Maisie lifted the pot off the stove and turned off the flame. She cut a lump of yeast and dropped it into the warm, golden liquid. "Jealous is the last thing Vince is." She picked up her spoon and started to swirl the yeast to dissolve it. "What did you want to tell me about Tom?"

"Okay." Ellie inhaled. "Tom's in love with Em. Cate's Em."

"What?" Maisie froze. "No way!"

"Yep." Ellie nodded. "I *know*."

Maisie put the spoon down. This needed her undivided attention. "He said that? To *you*?"

Ellie pulled a curl of hair over her shoulder and started to twirl it. "He didn't say it in those words. But he wanted me to know."

"Goodness. I think I need a second." Maisie wasn't sure how she felt about the news. She'd always believed Emily loved Alex. It'd been a huge disappointment when Alex had started dating Brandie instead of Em, though Maisie had made sure not to share that with her son.

Of course Maisie didn't want Em to be celibate in honor of his memory, or pine after the past. Not at all. But *Tom*?

Tom had been Alex's best friend, his wingman. A little older, a little wiser than Alex and Em. A big brother who had their backs. Then again, now that she thought about it...

"Tom's never dated anyone," they both said in unison, and then they had to laugh because of it.

"I didn't see it coming," Maisie admitted. "What exactly did Tom say?"

"He thinks Em can be happy in Beach Cove. He wants her to stay and figure things out."

"Hmm." Em was up against a lot in Beach Cove. Allen, for one. A lack of fulfilling jobs. Em was smart, and Maisie had always thought she'd fly the nest as soon and far as she could. "She's already working at the Café, isn't she?" Maisie started to sift flour into a bowl. There wasn't much else Tom could do to keep Em, other than pop the question.

"You should've seen me suggesting Becky instead." Ellie shook her head. "You'd have thought I said it to offend him."

"Who's Becky?"

Ellie sighed. "Her nana used to make blueberry cobbler for the fair. Anyway, Tom wants Em to create something she'll be proud of."

"Like what?"

"He wants Em to open a bakery."

"Oh! That's big. Beach Cove's never had a bakery."

"Well…" Ellie cleared her throat like a big lump lodged in it.

Maisie stopped sifting and looked at her friend. "Well what, Ells?"

"I've given Tom the Fish Market to turn into that bakery." Her lips kept moving after the last word, as if she was saying more.

Maisie set the bag of flour down and put a hand on her hip. "You've gone get rid of the fishery, Ells?"

The grammatical misstep did what it needed to do; Ellie chuckled. "I have indeed, uh…gone get rid of it. Yes."

They were silent for a moment, each processing their thoughts. Then Maisie went and pulled Ellie into a dusty white hug. "You did good, Ells. The fishes were your way to escape an unhappy marriage. That belongs to the past. We have the inn to keep us busy now, and the kids get the bakery they want. Maybe they'll even find love in the bargain. You did good."

"Thanks," came Ellie's muffled voice. "I can't breathe."

Maisie squeezed her friend and then returned to her bowl to pour the yeast into the flour and start kneading the dough. After a moment, she shook her head in disbelief. "Can you imagine?"

Ellie patted flour off her navy T-shirt. "Not really," she admitted. "Also, Em doesn't know yet. At this point, it's all in Tom's head."

Maisie nodded thoughtfully. "Tell him to be

patient. Em might not realize right away what an opportunity this is."

Unless you came from a long line of fisherfolk, there were few jobs in Beach Cove. For young people growing up, it was either creating their own opportunity or leaving in search of employment.

"We'll see how it goes. Em's an independent spirit," Ellie said.

"So she is." Maisie smiled. "You'd be lucky to get her for a daughter-in-law."

"A girl can dream, can't she? Little Tommys and Emmys running all over Beach House... Wouldn't that be something?"

"I'd love that. But go easy, Ells. It's a far way to think ahead. Does Em even know Tom likes her?"

"I don't exactly think so," Ellie said. "You know what?" She straightened suddenly. "Are you okay serving tea by yourself? There's cream in the fridge."

"Where are you going?" Maisie stopped kneading the dough. She'd looked forward to cake on the patio. If Ellie wasn't there to taste them too, the lemon tarts wouldn't be as sweet.

"I'm just going to go over and check on Cate real quick," Ellie called, already half out the door. "I keep forgetting Allen's back."

Chapter 20

"This is where you live?" Helene stood in the living room, clutching a Birkin bag.

Suddenly, Cate saw her house through Helene's eyes. The couch with the loose threads the cat had pulled, the coffee table that needed wiping. A cobweb, smudges on the wall.

"Yes, this is it," Cate said, resisting the urge to apologize. There was no reason to be embarrassed. It was a modest Cape Cod in Beach Cove, not a modern glass and steel construction in the hills of Hollywood.

An upstairs door banged, and Claire thundered down the stairs in lacrosse gear and ponytail, overnight duffel in arms.

"Claire, come here a moment. I haven't seen you in days."

"Hi, Mom." Claire came, slinging an arm around Cate's waist. "What's up?"

"This is your aunt Helene," Cate said without preamble. She couldn't think of one.

"My aunt Helene?" Claire shook her head. "What aunt Helene?"

Cate threw Helene an apologetic look. Of course

she'd told the girls about her sister. But there hadn't been much to say—and it seemed what little she had shared, Claire had forgotten. "Helene's my younger sister, Claire," she said.

"Oh!" Claire's eyes widened, but she caught herself, shifted the bag in her arms and held out her hand. "It's so nice to meet you, Aunt Helene."

Cate noticed that Helene's fingers trembled as she reached for her niece. "It's nice to meet you too, Claire." They shook and smiled.

"Um, Mom." Claire pulled her hand away again. "I have to get to practice. I'm going to stay with Em afterward. She said Grace and Zoe can come too, and tomorrow we'll all have breakfast at the Café together. Any chance I can take your car?"

"Sure." It would shock Helene, Cate thought, that her seventeen-year-old didn't even own her own vehicle. She pulled the keys from her purse and handed them to Claire. "Have fun, sweetheart. Make sure you girls let Em get some sleep. She's got to work tomorrow."

"Thank you! You're the best!" Claire pressed a kiss on Cate's cheek, waved at her newfound aunt and ran out the door.

Cate smiled. "She's always on the go."

"She's lovely," Helene said quietly. "If she ever needs an agent, I'd have no trouble placing her."

"Don't tell her," Cate joked. "She might just hop the midnight train to Los Angeles." But Cate knew Claire would do nothing like it. She was one of Beach Cove's bright young things and very much enjoyed her popularity and her friends.

Still looking after Claire, Helene slowly turned the diamond on her finger as if the ring hurt her.

"Would you like a cup of tea?" Cate asked gently.

"No, thank you," Helene said, straightening. "Can I see the yard?"

"Of course." Cate hadn't weeded in weeks, but when she opened the door, she thought the jumble of overgrown shrubs and wildflowers looked cheerful. She often sat out here with the girls, enjoying the peace and tranquility. Allen never came.

"Oh dear." Helene looked around but didn't step outside. "Don't you have help, Cate?"

Cate pursed her lips, a little hurt that her sanctuary had been so casually dismissed. "We used to have a babysitter when the girls were little, but it was expensive. There's no reason to pay for things we can do ourselves." She shrugged, trying not to look at the floor. Claire's cleats had left bits of soil and blades of grass. "We try to keep up."

"Did you say you're taking a sabbatical?"

"Yes. Come to the kitchen." Cate closed the door so the bugs wouldn't come in. "I'll make myself a cup of tea if you don't mind."

Cate needed something to hold on to. Talking with Helene had become much easier, but they were so different. There were still little barbs in their words.

Helene followed her and sat at the kitchen table. Cate put the kettle on the stove. "It'll be nice, having a year at home," she said to keep talking.

"You don't like teaching?"

"I like it very much." Cate felt her face flush. She missed the kids. She even missed the other teachers.

"Why are you taking off then?" Helene sounded confused. "Are you writing a book?"

"No." Cate looked at the floor. A blueberry had rolled under the sink, and she picked it up and tossed it. "Allen wants me to spend more time at home."

"Why?"

Cate exhaled. "He's going to be busy with new projects. He wants to make sure everything runs smoothly when he's gone. You know. The girls."

"Claire's the younger one? She seems pretty independent. How's the older one? Emily, right?"

"Yes, Em. She's just moved out. She doesn't live here anymore."

Helene narrowed her eyes. "Then what are you supposed to do, stand in the kitchen just in case he wants soup? Don't you need the money from your job?"

From the way she emphasized *need*, it was clear Helene thought Cate could do with the money.

"I'm still getting some money. Benefits too." Cate felt too warm. She shrugged, uncomfortable. "I don't want tea anymore." She turned off the fire and shifted the kettle.

"Who's asking why my wife stopped working?"

Cate's head jerked up. There stood Allen, leaning against the jamb of the kitchen door, staring at Helene.

"Oh, Allen!" she said hastily. "This is Helene. She's visiting Beach Cove."

"Yeah." Allen crossed his arms. "I remember you. You made Cate come to the hospital so her mother could kick up a stink and take her out of the will."

"Our mother was *dying*." Helene stood; her fine eyebrows sunk low. "Cate had a right to say goodbye. But you couldn't bear sharing her even for that. You were too scared she might come to her senses and leave you."

The heat in Cate's cheeks iced over. "No, Helene. That's not how it was."

Helene ignored her. "And now you're making her stay home to isolate her even more. What's next? Alienating her friends? Or have you started already?"

Allen pushed off the jamb. "Cate?" His voice was frosty. "Get her out of the house."

"Allen—she's my sister," Cate protested. "Please…"

Allen widened his eyes at Cate as if he couldn't understand why she didn't obey.

"Don't, Cate." Helene picked up her bag. "You've given me a lot to think about in the last days. I did take it to heart. But now it's your turn." She jerked her chin at Allen. "If what you say about Mother is true, then you've stumbled out of the frying pan and into the fire marrying Allen."

"What do you mean? No. No." Cate clasped her hands. She hoped her sister would shrug and leave, but Helene didn't stop.

"You husband's an abuser," she said matter of fact; as if it was the most obvious thing in the world. "He's isolated and manipulated you, and now he's tightening his net. You better get out while you still can."

Cate's eyes flew to Allen. "No—you two have gotten off on the wrong foot," she managed to get out. "It's not like that."

"You're so scared of him you can barely talk." Helene tilted her head. "Is he making you wear those ugly skirts?"

"No..." Yes, they were Allen's skirts. Cate liked loose overalls, light colors, flowy dresses and short skirts. Even if her legs were ugly.

Helene put her hands on Cate's shoulders. "I've watched beautiful, talented, smart women go through this," she said quietly. "I listened to you talk about Mother and the pattern of narcissistic abuse. I researched it at night, and I read. Listen to me now, Cate. You're still in the pattern. You're still in it. I'm only unhappy—but you're in danger."

She grabbed Cate's shoulders more firmly. "Remember what you told me? I'm telling you the same. Cate, you're my sister. I care."

Helene let go. Pushing past Allen without acknowledging him, she left.

Before the door fell shut, Ellie's voice called out. "Hey! Cate! You in there?"

Cate saw Allen clench his hand into a fist. "I don't want any more of your friends in my house," he hissed.

"It's all right," Cate whispered. She didn't have air for more. He'd never forgive her for what Helene had said. "I'm so sorry. I'll sort this out."

She hurried to the door, hoping to get Ellie to step

outside with her instead of coming in. But when she rounded the corner, Ellie was already pulling the front door shut behind her.

"I just saw Helene run out. She looked upset." Ellie frowned. "Are you okay? Did something happen?"

Behind her, Cate heard Allen's step; he'd followed her. "Everything's fine!" she said in a voice too high, too breathy. "I'm sorry I didn't text back, Ellie. I just forgot."

Ellie glanced at Allen. Cate didn't know what face he was making at her friend, but she hoped he'd hang on just a little longer before he blew up. She didn't want Ellie to see.

Ellie looked back, searching her face. Cate gave the tiniest shake of her head.

Ellie nodded. "No problem, Cate. You know what? I'll catch up later, okay?" She lowered her voice. "*Call me.*"

"Yes. Thank you," Cate said, full of gratitude. She just needed time to calm Allen down. "I promise. I'll call soon."

"Do it." Ellie gave her a warning look. She wasn't kidding around. Ellie was worried, and Cate knew she'd call everyone before pulling out of the driveway, so the girls would be on standby.

"Oh, look." Ellie stopped in the door and turned. Allen gave an impatient huff. "Is that the car you've been talking about?" she asked.

"Are they back?" Cate lifted on tiptoes to see over Ellie's head. She hadn't forgotten about the stalkers.

Suddenly, Allen was behind her, pushing Cate

into Ellie, peering out the door. "You've seen that car before?" he asked.

"Once or twice," Cate said. "So sorry, Ells, I didn't mean to bump you."

"No worries." Ellie wiggled out, jumped down the stairs and started walking to her car. "Let me know, Cate!"

"Let you know what?" Allen growled. But his eyes were still on the sedan parked opposite their house. A pale oval in the tinted window stared back.

Ellie pulled out her phone as she got into her car, and Cate wanted to wave, but Allen had grabbed her wrist—hard—and was pulling her back into the house, slamming the door shut.

"Ow!" she protested. "Allen! That hurts."

He let go with a sneer, tossing her hand so it made her shoulder ache. "Don't worry," he spat. "I wouldn't touch you even if you weren't so fat."

Cate rubbed her wrist, blinking at the floor. Allen had many ways of telling her she wasn't attractive, but it was always covert, hidden in the forest of his words. He'd never openly insulted her.

This was payback for what Helene had said. Cate held her breath, thanking her lucky star the kids weren't home. There'd be more.

Allen blew out an angry breath, but when he talked, his normal voice was back. "You're a real piece of work, Cate, making me say things like that. That car out there—you said you saw it before. How often? Why didn't you tell me?"

"I didn't think it would interest you," Cate

stammered. She felt stupid. She should've thought it through. She should've told Allen.

"Has it ever occurred to you it might be someone looking for me?"

It hadn't occurred to her. "Why would they—you think it's because of the shop window?"

He took a moment to answer. "Yes, because of the window. It might be reporters, waiting to take me down."

"Reporters? Really?" Cate tried to take a deep breath and somehow, the oxygen unhooked her brain. She could think again.

It was so unlikely, wasn't it? Allen wasn't famous. The public wasn't interested in his career. The media didn't care.

Allen was shutting down in front of her, like a machine that had burned all its fuel. The eyes hardened, the mouth stilled, the shoulders pulled back. Without another look or word, he left.

Cate heard the bedroom door close. The bolt clicked shut, and then the suitcase was dragged out from under the bed and over the floor.

Chapter 21

"Check this out." Em stepped back. She hadn't called Tom to come admire her coconut cake. She wasn't bothering him. He'd walked into her space all by himself, and so she was well within her rights to ask his opinion.

Tom leaned over her shoulder, each hand holding a ball of pizza dough. He smelled of oregano and thyme and the same laundry detergent he'd used since high school.

"Looks good enough to eat," he said into her ear, and she had to giggle and rub it because his peppermint breath tickled. "What's that on top?"

"Roasted coconut shavings," Em said. "Sorry for hogging the stovetop."

"Mikey's still livid. Hang on." Tom left to plop the dough on the pizza counter, then checked the oven temperature and nodded at Mikey, the teen who was helping with chopping and washing. "These need to rise. Give them five minutes and start kneading, okay?"

Em heard Tom return. "Oops!" She'd almost bumped into him when she turned—she'd not realized he was so close already. "Sorry again."

Tom shook his head: nobody got hurt. "Do you have a minute?"

"Well…" Em threw a longing look at the bowl with the kitchen towel. The middle bulged into a soft dome, and she'd been looking forward to punching the dough down. But it would keep. She nodded. "What's up, boss?"

"Stop calling me that." Tom took her hand. "Come with me. I want to talk."

"Okay." Em followed as he led her out back into the alley, carefully closing the door behind him. Either he had a key on him, or they'd be stuck walking back in through the front.

She eyed him curiously.

Tom was dressed in a pink shirt and jeans, front covered by the same long apron Em was wearing herself. It wasn't noon yet, and already the fabric showed plentiful proof of his work. Specks of marinara and smudges of flour; badges of honor for a chef. But not how he usually showed himself to his guests.

Em wasn't much better; she was wearing jeans and a slinky T-shirt that fell off one shoulder. Fell off a lot more than she'd realized in the store's changing cabin. Her own frosting-speckled apron held things together, but she wasn't customer-ready either.

Tom reached below his bib, patting his chest.

"Hey!" Em realized what he was doing. "You promised to stop!"

"Sorry." He flashed her an apology. "I will. I swear.

Just not right now. I've got too much going on." He reached into the hidden breast pocket and pulled out a pack of cigarettes, shaking one out and lighting up in one smooth motion. "I won't blow smoke in your direction. See?" Tom took a long pull, then blew the vapor out straight up into the air. He closed his eyes.

"I'm not going to watch you kill yourself." Em, who'd sat on the step, rose. "I've got buns to make."

"Em, forget the smoking for a second, okay? I'll take care of it, I promise. It's my only sin, so cut me a little slack. I'll stop. Soon."

Em sat back down again. Usually, Tom was the one who was relaxed and easygoing. But not now. He was stressed about something, and she could tell he wanted to talk about it. "What's up, Tom?" She squished her lips together, trying unsuccessfully to ignore the cigarette in his hand. He'd *promised*.

He leaned against the metal railing. "How do you like work so far, Em?"

"Oh." She hadn't expected to have to report already. It'd only been a few days. "So far, so good. I like it. Why?" She pulled her shirt higher. "Has someone complained about the passionfruit cake? Was it too extra? I'm still learning."

"No, no." He took another couple of long draws and then pressed the butt into a tin can full of rainwater he'd pulled out from under the stairs. Em heard the hiss as it went out. Tom pushed the can back, then straightened and ran his hands through his hair.

"It's going to smell like cigarette smoke now," Em

observed.

He dropped his hands in an open-palmed so-what gesture. "Nobody cares."

"I care. Let me check." She went to him and stood on tiptoes, smelling his hair. She'd expected him to laugh and push her away, but he didn't.

"Okay, fine, you smell good enough," she conceded and went back to her spot. Something was different. Maybe he didn't like his employees sniffing him. Probably.

"Thank you, Mother." He sighed, and then he sat beside her on the stair. "Scooch over."

There were plenty of other stoops, and it was a little crowded, shoulder pressing into shoulder. But Em didn't mind. It meant she'd been forgiven for sniffing her boss.

"So what did you want to tell me?" she asked politely.

"Well, see, I asked the customers how they liked the cake the last few days."

"Uh-oh. One of those where you go around all official and ask while they're eating?"

"Exactly. Like that. And they said..."

"What? What did they say?"

He grinned. "They said it was okay."

Em felt her face fell. "Oh. Oh no."

Tom bumped her with his shoulder. "No, of course not, Em. They said it was the best they'd ever had, except for my raspberry roll. That one hit it out of the ballpark, though to be honest, I think it's mostly due to hear-say. But they loved the passionfruit, and everything else got high praise too. I mean, *high* praise."

"Ooh." Em blew out a tense breath. "Really?"

He put an arm around her and briefly pulled her into him before letting go. "Yes, really, Em. You're a good baker."

"I can do better. I'll try tiramisu rolls next; I've been waiting for a chance to work at the pizza counter because it's longer." The words bubbled out of her. "I think I could squeeze in just before noon if Mikey uses the table for the garlic knots. What do you think?"

It took Tom a moment to respond. "There'd be a problem with the oven temperature. We need to jack up the heat for the roast at noon. Tiramisu would burn. And after the roast, it's pizza time. Not enough space then, and still too hot."

"Oh. Right." Em felt stupid. She'd not been watching the kitchen routine closely enough. "Well, maybe in a couple of weeks... You're not planning on keeping the roast on the menu, do you?"

"I don't know. There've been more orders last week, so I should keep it on longer."

"Oh," Em said again. It was stupid to be disappointed; she knew that. There was still plenty she could bake. But she'd been looking forward to trying out the new recipes she'd squirreled into a folder on her computer. And the tiramisu roll had looked so tempting; one hundred percent, it'd be as much a hit as Tom's raspberry.

"I had coffee with my mom yesterday," Tom said out of the blue.

"Yeah?" Suddenly, Em felt tired. She'd been up early every day since working with Tom, starting even before he came in to prove she was worth her salary. Em leaned her head against his shoulder. "What did you guys talk about?"

"She's happy with the Beach Cove Inn. She thinks it'll make money, too."

"It should. It's beautiful, and a gazillion people are trying to book a room. I totally would if I could afford it." Em smiled, thinking about Ellie in the grand old mansion by the sea. She deserved to call it home, especially after what her ex-husband had done to her. And Tom.

She laid a hand on his arm. Poor Tom.

Beside her, Tom drew in a long, audible breath. "Yeah. She said she'd like to put more time and energy into the inn. They want to make a real go of it."

"What about the Fish Market?"

"That's what I'm saying."

Em straightened to see his face. "I don't understand. Does she want you to work there?" No, of course not; Ellie was too proud of the Corner Café. Did Ellie want Em for the job? Was Tom telling her she was going to sell fish from now on? Em put a hand to her heart. Oh, no... She wanted to keep doing *this*. Bake. Have back alley talks with her best friend.

"In a way." Tom's eyes held hers. He had heterochromia, which in his case looked like shifting eye color. Sometimes, his irises were more green. In this light, Em thought they looked very blue.

"She's selling me the building," Tom said.

Em nodded, mute. It'd been too fun to last. "So you're doing fish, too?"

"I'm going to turn it into a bakery, Em," he said. "But I can't do it on my own because I'm needed at the Corner Café."

"A bakery!" She felt her eyes widen at the same time her spine stiffened. "And so..." She cleared her throat. "Uh. Would you mind telling me again? I mean, all of it. Full sentences."

He smiled. "I'm hoping you'll run the bakery. I want us to be partners."

"Wait." Em covered her face with her hands. "What? *Partners*?" she said through her fingers.

"Yes. I finance, you run it, we split the profit." Tom reached out, pulling a hand off her face and into his own. He rubbed her palm with his thumb. "What do you think?"

Em couldn't think. Her brain was like the soft yeast dough waiting in the bowl; wobbly and waiting to collapse. "I don't know."

What did it mean, running a bakery? All by herself? What did she need to do? Was Tom going to be involved at all? She liked having him around. Could she even—

"Hey." He took her other hand too. "It's okay. You don't have to do it. Honest."

"I don't..." Em drew a breath. "I'm like, what?" She laughed, embarrassed. "I don't know how to run a bakery, Tom. What do I do?"

"You plan what you want to bake. You order the things you need," Tom said. His voice was calm, as if it was no problem. "If I can do it, you can do it too. You're the smart one, remember?"

Em rolled her head to relax her neck muscles. Okay. She could order sugar and flour and cherries and eggs. Chocolate, too. Yes.

"You keep a record of what things cost and what you spend. You'll bake in the morning. During the day, you'll help customers and see what sells. When you're out, you're out, and you make a bigger batch next time. Once we get going, we'll adjust the plan as needed."

Em's brain settled, holding on to the structure. Tom made it sound possible. "And you?" she asked. "What do you do?"

"I do the rest." He smiled. There was probably quite a lot to 'the rest,' Em thought. "The taxes and the legal stuff's my bit, so don't worry about it for now. It's really not so complicated, and you can do it yourself when you're ready. But for starters, you mostly bake. In your own space. On proper counters and your own ovens."

"In the Fish Market?" She didn't want to sound ungrateful. But there wasn't an oven, only freezers and fridges.

"We'll renovate. Turn it into a cozy bakery, the sort that sells people their morning bagels. We can have one of those self-serve coffee machines that also make cappuccinos and cocoa and tea. We can put in a few tables inside and a couple of bistro sets outside so people can sit and have their cake."

"Or muffins. And chocolate croissants."

He let go of her hands. "You've got it."

"And also, uh…"

Tom laughed and ran a hand through his hair. He looked happier now. "Yeah, we'll definitely have to talk more. Maybe…" He stood. "Can you stay after the Café closes? We could have dinner and make plans."

"That sounds lovely." Em stood as well. She felt her chest expanding, her lungs drawing in air. This was big. This was *big*. It was the next beginning; she could feel it in her blood. "Goodness, Tom," she said, hugging herself. "If only Alex could be here with us now, right?"

Tom turned away, looking at the clouds above the alley. "Yes," he said, his voice low. "I wish he could be. I wonder how things would be if he were."

"Me, too." Em patted the stair crud off her jeans, biting her lip. "Hey, I'd better go back in."

She'd put her foot in, bringing up their lost friend. Some time, they'd talk about it. All of it. Alex, how much Tom missed him, the pink shirt, how it could be difficult to come out in a town as small as Beach Cove. But now was not the time.

Em wished she'd kept her big mouth shut. A moment ago, they'd been so joyful about the bakery. "Are you coming?" she asked quietly.

"You go ahead," Tom said, his back still to her. "I'll be there in a sec."

Emily jumped up the stairs. The sweet yeast dough, warm and soft and scented, was waiting. "Hey," she said and stopped. "The door's closed."

"Here. Just leave it open a notch." Tom handed

her the key. Already waiting in his hand was another cigarette.

"Really, Tom?"

"Just one." He sighed. "Go on ahead. I need a minute."

"Hmm." She really shouldn't have mentioned Alex. Tom still felt so much guilt about his disappearance and death. Like it'd been his fault when it'd just been a terrible, stupid accident. Em wished she could bring Tom back to a good place. *Their* place. The bakery.

She let herself in, casting a last glance at her best friend. She couldn't stand it when he was sad. Sometimes, it felt like he was all she had. "I love you, Tommy."

"Yeah, I know. Love you too, Emmy." Standing with his back to the door, Tom lit a match. His head hunched over the flame.

Em put the key on the stair so he could use it later. Then she shut the door.

Chapter 22

"In a way, this is nice." Helene took her wedges off and set them next to the boardwalk that had led them through dunes to the beach.

"Sure," Cate said. The afternoon sky was cloudy, and the sea was gray, but it looked beautiful.

"At first I didn't like it," Helene admitted. "The beaches in Southern California are busy and bright. Here they are lonely and rugged and half the time it's so foggy you can't even see where you're going. It's almost as if the sea is playing games with you. But it's starting to grow on me. I'm starting to think it's got a certain romance."

Cate's eyes traced the gentle curve of the coast. She didn't see anything lonely or rugged in the smooth, white sand, other than maybe the strip of bleached driftwood and kelp that'd washed ashore. But the beach did look romantic. Like something from a movie.

Especially when new fog was coming in as it did now. Vapor swirled over the waves and spread a thin veil across the sand. Plovers, their legs already hidden, floated like nervous little clouds along the waterline.

Maybe Cate could find a sand dollar or a piece of sea glass. She'd set it in a necklace for her sister, even though Helene would never wear it. Still, it'd be a little keepsake to look at and remember the visit.

Having looked her fill, Helene stepped onto the sand. Cate slipped out of her sandals and followed. The sand was cool and gritty with moisture under her bare feet.

"Is Allen okay?" Cate felt Helene's glance. "I hope I didn't get you in trouble."

Cate considered a little laugh. But it would be fake, and of course Helene would notice. "It's all right," she said. "He was angry. At me, not at you."

"I'm the one who told him off. You didn't do anything." Helene walked faster. They'd reached the water, and the first wave spilled warm and soft over Cate's toes. It was one of the best feelings she knew.

"Allen's just...like that," Cate said. "He thinks I provoked you. He doesn't like being called an abuser, you know."

"I bet he doesn't," Helene said drily, and then she stopped sloshing through the water. "Why is this so hard, Cate? I still have trouble believing you when you talk about Mother. In my head I know—" She fell quiet.

Cate felt the effort it cost her younger sister to speak again; it was as if the air around her thickened with it.

"I know at least some of the things you say are true." Unseeing, Helene stared at the water. "I know you didn't eat Aunt Jane's muffin because I did. I remember seeing Mother unravel her knitting herself, though I thought it was a dream. And I know you weren't sleeping around in high school. There wasn't much I didn't know about in Stoning High."

"You always were popular." Mother had worked hard on Helene's outfits, her hair and social schedule, to catapult her to the top of the school trendsetters.

"I never wanted to be," Helene replied and started walking again. "I didn't enjoy being popular, even though I didn't realize it. It was like I was a train on tracks I had to follow, whether I liked it or not. There wasn't a choice."

"Not until much later. And then you came to talk with me. I appreciate your courage, Helene."

"I'm still compelled to be the popular girl wherever I go."

"I'm sure it's hard to let go. It's hard to tell what's Mother and what is you."

"I suppose the line was never drawn properly." Helene sounded as if she were sleep talking. Flat and hollow. "Maybe that's what's next for me. Drawing that line."

Cate wanted to embrace Helene; tell her she was proud of her. But they hadn't yet reached a level of familiarity that allowed for easy hugs. "Good luck, little sister," Cate finally said. "I already know who you are. You'll be so happy when you find out for yourself."

Helene stepped out of the way of a wave. "I'm worried about you," she said. "Because of Allen."

"Don't be worried," Cate said mechanically. She'd pretended for so long her marriage was all right her brain went numb thinking about it. "We're working on it."

"Well, don't." Helene rubbed her neck. "You should let go as well. Sometimes, you need to stop working and get out."

"But we're—" Almost, Cate repeated, 'working on it,' catching herself just in time. "Uh. Yes. I'll see."

"Why *can't* you see?" Helene raised her hands in frustration. "You recreated what you thought you'd left behind. You know Mother lied about who you are, but the knowledge is all in your head."

Helene stopped, and to Cate's utter surprise, knocked a knuckle against Cate's collarbone. It made a dull sound which Cate heard from the inside of her body.

"You don't feel it in your heart who you are," Helene said. "You still feel you're not good enough. You feel you don't deserve love. Worse, you feel you deserve hate. That's why you allow Allen to treat you the way he does."

Cate brushed Helene's hand away. This was going too far. "I don't—He doesn't *hate* me."

"He hates everybody. But he blames you. It's easy for him because you're already used to it."

Cate frowned. "He *doesn't*—"

"Who's that?" Helen shaded her eyes against the diffuse glare reflecting off the haze. "A man. He's waving."

Cate squinted. "Oh no." Her heart dropped like an elevator. "It's Calvin." Not now. Not here. She felt stressed, as if Helene had just attacked her.

She didn't want to hear what her sister was

saying. Because what if Helene was right? Had Cate really recreated a situation where she once again was the victim of a narcissistic abuser?

"Hello there," Calvin called.

"Hi," Cate called back, trying to sound cheerful. The last time they'd met, he'd introduced Cate to his ex-wife Sarah. It'd been in the summer, and Cate had thought of him often. She didn't want to be gloomy now that she finally saw him again.

They came to a stop with only a few yards between them. Cate blinked, trying not to stare. He was still the same, but her eyes grazed over every detail, his eyes, his nose, the clothes he wore, as if her brain had been starved for a refresher.

"Uh, Helene, this is Calvin McMurphy. Calvin, this is my sister Helene Terry."

There it was, the admiring glance Cate was so used to seeing when she introduced Helene to men.

"Nice to meet you, Helene." Calvin smiled at Helene, who returned the smile in a rather uninterested way.

Cate wanted to say something more. "Calvin's the local pharmacist."

He looked at her in his deadpan way. Usually, he had a funny comment for her, sometimes even a compliment. But nothing came, and Cate clasped her hands, willing herself not to look away.

How stupid of her, that sense of loss. She'd sent him away; told him she wasn't interested. It'd been months. Of course he had found someone else, or at least forgotten all about Cate.

But at one time, he had been interested in her. He had been eager to know her.

"Not for much longer," Calvin said.

"What?" Cate leaned forward. She'd missed something.

"I might not be the local pharmacist much longer." He broke their eye contact. "This is a goodbye walk, to be honest. I'm leaving Beach Cove tomorrow."

"Oh no!" The words escaped Cate too loud for the quiet, foggy afternoon. Louder than even the rushing of the sea.

Calvin looked back at her, and from the corner of her eye, Cate saw Helene glance over too.

Cate cleared her throat, embarrassed. "Why would you leave Beach Cove?"

"Because..." Calvin clasped his hands behind his back. "Life here didn't work out the way I'd hoped."

"Is business bad?" How could it be? She'd been so sure he was doing great. "Every time I walk by the pharmacy, it seems to burst with customers."

"Well." When he spoke, his words came carefully, tiptoeing into sentences. "I hit an unexpected turn in the road, Cate. I can't get past it, so the plan is to check in with some good friends and come up with a solution. Tomorrow, I'll drive to Vermont. I've always wanted to see the fall in Vermont."

Cate's brain buzzed with confusion. "But the leaves haven't yet turned." It was too early for Vermont. Wasn't it?

Helene tilted her head. "Are you selling the local pharmacy?"

He looked at her. "Are you interested in purchasing it?"

"I'm starting to like it here, and I understand real estate pickings are slim." Helene reached into her pocket and handed Calvin a card.

He took it with it a nod.

"I'm so sorry," Cate said. She couldn't buy his pharmacy. She couldn't go to Vermont with him or offer to be his confidante so he could tell her his troubles. "Is there anything I can do?" she asked helplessly.

Calvin's chest expanded as if he was going to say something, a lot, but then he shook his head. "I don't think you can, Cate." His words were barely audible over the waves, as if the sea wanted to drown them out. "But it's kind of you to offer."

"Hmm." Cate wanted to know more; she wanted to know what his troubles were. And where exactly Calvin was going. Was he traveling alone? Or would the charming Sarah come along? Cate liked Sarah very much. But she couldn't help feeling a jealous sting, thinking Calvin would explore Vermont with his radiant ex by his side.

"How are things with you, Cate?" Calvin asked.

"Fine," she said automatically.

"Not fine," Helene butted in. "You're not fine at all."

"Helene!"

"What's going on, Cate?" Calvin's eyebrows drew together.

Cate gestured that it was nothing.

"Why aren't you honest with your friends, Cate?" Helene demanded. "Tell them how Allen treats you!"

Cate opened her mouth but was actually speechless. Not in front of Calvin.

"What does Allen do?" Calvin asked. He didn't look deadpan anymore. His brow furrowed sharp as a knife between his blue eyes. "What's going on, Cate?"

"Nothing!" Cate snapped her mouth shut and glared at Helene. "Nothing's going on. Helene! Don't go telling strangers stories about me!"

Calvin shook his head as if she'd smacked him, and Cate slapped a hand over her mouth. "I'm sorry! I'm sorry, Calvin."

"No—no. You're right." Calvin took a step to the side, away from them. "Of course we're strangers. The last time we talked is months ago, isn't it? It's none of my business what's going on in your life."

Cate shook her head, miserable. Calvin was a stranger to Helene. That's what she'd meant.

He wasn't a stranger to Cate. "I'm sorry," she said again.

Beside her, Helene had fallen silent.

"No, I shouldn't have... Well, bye." Calvin took another couple of steps to the side. He was higher on the beach now, his path clear of them.

"Have a good trip, Calvin." Cate felt like crying.

She'd offended him. They were more than strangers, more than even acquaintances. Much more. The words were on the tip of her tongue.

He stood for a heartbeat or two as if he was waiting for them, then he nodded and started to walk, his feet shifting the wet sand.

Cate had not wanted it to end like that. She'd always wanted—more. Their story hadn't ended. Despite her resolution to stay with Allen, she'd always thought Calvin would be there. In Beach Cove. And somehow, part of her life.

Helene put a hand on her arm, and Cate flinched.

"I apologize," Helene said. "I misread the situation. I really thought you two were good friends. I'm sorry I embarrassed you, Cate."

"Yeah, well." Cate swallowed the lump in her throat, but it kept raising. "He's... It's just I didn't know he was leaving. It's... I just didn't know."

"It's okay," Helene said. She took Cate's arm and led her back toward the boardwalk. Far ahead, Cate saw Calvin, still walking away from her.

"Let's have a cup of something warm," Helene said. "Can we go to your house? Is Allen home?"

Cate tried to think. "He left last night for a seminar. Or a workshop? A company called and asked if he could do one on short notice. They promised to pay extra. We need the money."

"Good," Helene let go of Cate's arm and bent to put her wedges back on. "Listen, I'm going to stay with you tonight, all right? I'll cook. Let me make it up to you."

"Okay." Soon, Helene would leave. They should spend their remaining time together. But really, Cate wanted Sam, Maisie, Ellie. A bottle of chardonnay and her friends.

"Okay." Helene took Cate's hand as if she were a

little kid, leading her up the boardwalk and back to the car.

Chapter 23

True to her word, Helene set to work; she rummaged through the fridge and cupboards in Cate's kitchen, pulling out chicken breast and tomatoes and tortillas, cheese and sour cream and cilantro. There was rice in the cupboard and a can of pinto beans Helene checked for expiration.

"Enchiladas Suizas," she announced. "Go ahead and call your friends while I cook. I know you want to."

Cate called Maisie to tell her about Calvin leaving, but once that was done, and they'd said what a pity it was to lose a nice person and a good pharmacist, there wasn't much else she or Maisie could add. Cate had told them long ago she wanted to work it out with Allen.

Instead, Maisie talked about Will, the inn's first guest. Will was polite, quite the joker, joined her and Ellie on the patio for afternoon tea but preferred to eat dinner with Vince.

Maisie and Ellie's menus and cooking skills rested uneasily. They were bored. Luckily, Vince had more friends, and arrangements for new visitors were being made.

"Calvin could stay at the inn too," Maisie said. "In case he ever wants to come back for a visit. You should let him know."

The thought depressed Cate. She didn't want Calvin to visit. She wanted him to belong to Beach Cove.

For a moment she regretted not having walked the middle. They didn't need to be lovers or strangers; they could've been friends. But then she remembered Calvin had said he didn't want to be friends.

She felt heat rise to her cheeks. Not so long ago, he'd liked her enough to refuse the friend zone.

"Dinner's ready," Helene's voice rang out, and Cate ended the call and went into the kitchen. Under normal circumstances, the smell of gold-brown cheese and warm tortillas would've made her mouth water. Now she didn't have an appetite.

"Smells delicious," she said dutifully and sat at the kitchen table. There were two plates, silverware, a kitchen towel for a napkin, a glass of ice water. She smiled; it looked exactly as if a sister had cooked for a sister. "Thank you for this, Helene."

"I can't remember the last time I cooked." Helene surveyed the table with a satisfied look. "But I think it's turned out pretty good." With hands swaddled in kitchen towels, she carried the casserole pan to the table.

"What do you eat if you don't cook?" Cate asked.

"I have a chef." Helene looked up, surprised. "He comes three times a week and prepares what I need.

Not much, usually. I have most of my meals with clients in restaurants."

It hadn't occurred to Cate that people employed personal chefs. Celebrities, sure. But normal people? "You're doing really well for yourself, aren't you?" she asked shyly.

Helene angled a slotted spoon into the pan and levered out a piece of casserole. "I do." She scooped the baked tortilla on Cate's plate, then helped herself. "There should be a salad to go with this, but I couldn't find any." She sat and looked expectantly at Cate.

Cate smiled and picked up her fork. She recognized the expectant look because Claire sometimes looked like that at Em. Em's approval meant everything to Claire. Nobody, not even Cate, could lift Claire like her older sister.

Cate cut a corner of the Enchilada Suizas and put it in her mouth. It was hot and— "Oh!" she said. The taste surprised her. It was fresh and full, as if the tomatoes and peppers had been hanging in the sun all day instead of sitting in the fridge. Even the cheese seemed more flavorful. "This is *good*, Helene. How did you do that?"

Helene beamed in triumph. Suddenly she looked exactly like Claire when Em had praised her riding skills at the end of horse camp.

It only lasted a moment. As soon as Helene met Cate's eyes, her features rearranged into the adult face. "What? Is there something on my chin?"

"Nope." Cate lowered her head to hide her smile. Claire and Em gave each other chin-warnings too.

Next, Helene would tell her to stop looking in her direction or breathe too loudly.

"Pretty good," Helene announced after tasting herself. "My cook taught me a thing or two."

"He did. I think Claire looks like you when you were sixteen."

"Does she?"

When they were done, Cate cleared the table while Helene went into the living room to check her messages and dictate emails into her phone. Cate listened, wondering about the curt, concise instructions her sister sent her employees. Not unkind, but unapologetic.

Cate filled the kettle and put it on the stove, then rummaged for tea bags. "Do you like rooibos tea?" she called out when there was a break in the dictation. "It's good with honey."

Helene appeared at the door, cell phone in hand. "No, thank you." She shook her perfect hair, too glamorous for tea.

Cate straightened. "How about a martini?"

"Um…okay. Can I make it?"

"What, you don't trust my cocktail-making skills?"

It barely was a joke, but Helene laughed out loud. "No. I don't trust your cocktail-making skills. You'll have to visit me sometime, Cate. I'll show you cocktail skills."

"Do you have a bartender as well?" Cate pointed at the liquor cabinet. The gin in there wasn't half bad. Supermarket, of course.

"As a matter of fact, I do. Often enough."

Cate pulled two glasses out and set them in front of Helene, who was inspecting the gin label. Her face was carefully neutral. Too neutral.

Cate could now tell what the little wrinkles and creases, the shapes of Helene's mouth and eyes meant. They came and went like flashes of light and dark, allowing insights into her mind. Cate was slow and sweet like Dad. Helene was sharp and quick like Mother.

"You don't have to drink it," Cate said kindly. "It's nothing special."

Helene looked up, squinting slightly as if she was measuring Cate up. She set the bottle on the kitchen counter. "No," she said. "It's fine. It doesn't always have to be special. I'll like it."

They had their drinks in the yard.

"I never feel like it's enough," Helene said. The evensong of a robin wove through her words. "I have everything you can think of, Cate. Everything. But it's like I'm still waiting for Mother to finally tell me it's good now. That I did well and may sit back and relax."

"She wanted more for you," Cate answered. But she knew that it wasn't the whole truth. To her surprise, Helene confirmed it.

"She wanted more for herself. It wasn't about me. It was all about herself. She was like a queen who always needed more power."

"Narcissism is a disease, Helene," Cate said. "I think she was ill. People talk about this person and that being a narcissist. But most of them aren't;

they're just a bit selfish. Mother was more. Remember the time she burned me?"

"No," Helene said. "Oh, no."

"She pretended it was an accident. But it wasn't." Cate still had the cigarette burn on her thigh. She'd never told the story, not even to Em. Mother had looked straight into her eyes, and the look had been worse than the pain. Cate breathed through the memory. "It's pathological," she repeated. "I'd say it wasn't her fault, but it's a fine line. I think she knew what she was doing the way an alcoholic knows they're drinking. It doesn't mean they can stop."

"You think it's the same?"

"I don't know. I like to think Mother would've preferred to be kind." Cate rubbed her thigh where the old scar was, pale and shiny.

Helene didn't respond.

Because what was there to say? In the end, there were only a person's actions and words. The things that were hidden, the things left undone and the words left unspoken, couldn't be measured.

"Let's forgive her," Cate said. "Whatever it was, let's think of it as an illness. She should've had help."

Helene nodded. "Yes. Let's forgive her." She glanced at Cate. "But I still want to understand."

"I know."

They emptied their glasses and carried them inside. Then Cate offered her sister the spare bedroom, and Helene accepted.

Cate brought towels and a bottle of water, a small blue vase with fall daisies for the nightstand, her best nightgown. "Sleep well," she said.

"You too." Helene smiled, looking at the folded nightgown in her hands. "I can't believe you sleep in this. I'll have to take you shopping."

Cate smiled back and shut the door quietly, then went downstairs to her own room, brushed her teeth and washed and put on a robe. It was early yet, but she felt drowsy after the rich food and strong drink. Too drowsy to tackle the stack of books by her bedside.

Instead, Cate laid on her bed and watched the light through the gossamer curtains fade from red to purple to cobalt.

Chapter 24

The fog was thinning, revealing the silhouette of a person walking toward Cate. A man, weaving to avoid the waves that nipped at the beach like hungry dogs.

Calvin?

But Calvin had left Beach Cove.

Cate squinted, but the smog was too thick to see. She wanted to swerve out of the way of the man. He'd run into her if she didn't move, but her feet had sunk into the wet sand. It sucked greedily, shackling her to the spot.

An arm materialized in the fog, and Cate's heart drummed against her ribs while she waited for the rest of the body to appear. But instead of ending in a torso, the arm grew longer and longer, its clasping hand reaching for Cate, clammy fingers closing around her wrist. Cate tried to scream, to writhe away, but she was stuck to her waist in quicksand.

A bird warbled.

Confused, the fingers on her wrist loosened.

The bird warbled again and again, in the repeating pattern that was Cate's ringtone.

Shaking the nightmare off, Cate groped for the

phone on the nightstand, pressing the correct key out of sheer habit.

"Mom?"

Cate pried her eyes open. It was dark outside the window. Only a skinny moon hung in the branches of the elm. "Em?"

"Sorry, Mom. Claire's knee hurts from playing lacrosse. Can she take Tylenol? There's a medication she's allergic to, isn't there? She says it's something else, but she can't remember what. I just want to make sure."

Cate pulled her cover higher, circling her free wrist and wiggling her toes. Nobody was holding her. She wasn't drowning in sand. "Tylenol is fine. Claire's allergic to amoxicillin. It's an antibiotic."

"I'll bring her to the doctor first thing tomorrow morning if it doesn't get better," Em promised. "Sorry if I woke you up; I was hoping you'd still be awake. Uh, are you all right? You sound weird."

"I..." Cate tried to swallow, but her throat was too dry. "It smells funny." She pushed the cover back. "Em, it smells funny. I'll call you back."

"What do you mean, it smells funny?" Em asked, alarmed.

"Go take care of your sister," Cate ordered. "I'll call you back."

Gripping her cell, she was about to switch on the bedside lamp when she froze. There was light shining in the gap below the door.

It wasn't steady like the hall light. It flickered and danced and smelled of—

"Fire," Cate whispered. Then she yelled, "Fire! There's a fire in the house! Helene!" She jumped out of bed. "Helene, get up!" Cate rushed to the door and yanked it open.

A wall of heat and smoke slammed into her like a cornered predator. Instinctively, Cate pulled her robe over her mouth and nose, and then she dove into the acrid fumes.

Helene was upstairs.

The fire billowed from the kitchen door, flames licking the living room, the bookshelf and couch and piano, but the stairs were still clear. Cate took them three, four at once. The smoke followed her like a malevolent spirit, despite the robe filling her nostrils and lungs.

"Helene!" Cate coughed.

The door to the guest room burst open; Helene stood on the threshold, Cate's gown flowing around her like a Victorian ghost. Her hair was mussed, her eyes wide, Birkin bag in her hand. "Get back down, Cate!" She too pulled her robe over her face.

"Come!" Cate turned and raced the stairs down, waiting at the bottom for her sister. Already, flames reached for the bottom stair, thrashing like a python. "Out! Come on, Helene!" Cate steered Helene through the toxic smoke.

They pulled open the front door and heard a whoosh behind them—the fire was roaring toward them, hungry for oxygen.

Cate grabbed Helene's hand and dragged her outside. They stumbled through the front yard into the road, where it was safe, and cool, and where they stood transfixed, chests heaving, coughing, staring at the burning house.

Lights flicked on in neighboring windows, doors banged, people ran out in bed-hair and pajamas. "I called nine one one!" someone yelled, and somebody else yelled they'd also called, and then Cate heard sirens singing through the night until they were engulfed in flashing lights and running men and trailing hoses and crashing windows; quick, are there any other people in the house? But Claire was safe at Em's, and someone ushered her and Helene into an ambulance, and then Sam was there, pulling Cate back out of the ambulance and into her arms.

"You're all right," Sam said, as hoarse as if she too had swallowed smoke. "You're all right, Cate."

Cate focused her eyes.

Time slowed again.

There was Sam. Behind Sam, firefighters hosed down the house, sending beams of water through black, gaping maws in the siding, straight into Cate's kitchen.

Sam let go of all but Cate's elbow as if she was scared Cate would fall.

Cate exhaled until she was empty. Then, slowly, carefully, she took a new breath. The clean air scratched her throat and singed her lung. She coughed.

"Ma'am. We need to check that out."

"I'm okay. Sorry. I'm fine. Thanks." Cate waved the first responder off. He was one of her old students.

"I still have to check."

"Liam." Adrenaline made Cate's voice rough, and the young man flinched as if he'd been caught passing notes. "I'm fine." She glanced over his shoulder. "Helene? How are you?"

Helene pulled an oxygen mask off her face, looking at it with an expression of disgust. "I don't need this." She gathered her hem in one hand and jumped out of the ambulance. "I'm fine too."

Cate could feel Sam bristle like a German shepherd. "You're Cate's sister," she said coldly. "I've heard about you." The fire truck lights turned Sam's white-blond hair red, then black, then back to red. She really did look witchy.

"Can I at least take your vitals, ma'am? I'm supposed to. You can also have a blanket and a bottle of water."

"No, thank you to all," Cate said, aware of the edge in her voice.

Liam mumbled something and excused himself.

"Bye," Cate called after him in a weak effort to restore civility. "Say hi to your Mom from me!"

He waved an acknowledgment.

"Sam," Cate said firmly. "Leave Helene be. She's fine. We're both fine."

Sam relaxed her stance. "The fire marshal said not to wait around. He knows how to find you. Come home with me. Or you can stay with Maisie and Ells. I already called them."

"I want to go to Beach House," Cate said at once. Beach House felt like the safe haven she needed.

"Gotcha." Sam scanned the night. "Hang on just one moment." She strode off with long legs and stiff knees.

Cate didn't know who Sam talked to, but it didn't take her long. "Okay," Sam called out when she came striding back. In her hand was Cate's phone; Cate hadn't even noticed she'd lost it.

"Beach House it is," Sam said and handed Cate the phone. "I texted Em. She said to call her the second you get somewhere warm and safe. Come on."

"Wait." Liam was back, waving a clipboard. "If you decline medical treatment, you have to sign these. Uh. Please, Mrs. Clark. If you would."

Cate took the pen and signed, then handed the clipboard to Helene, who also scribbled down her name. "Thanks, Liam. I didn't mean to yell. It was the shock."

Liam nodded. "No worries. I'll tell my mom you said hi, Mrs. Clark."

Sam had parked at the curb, some distance away. Neighbors were calling out to Cate as she passed, and she waved back, smiling as if her house going up in flames was just an unfortunate accident.

"You almost seem glad," Sam commented as she led the way to the truck.

"It's the shock," Helene said behind Cate. "She's in shock."

"No, I'm not." Cate slid into the passenger's seat of Sam's truck. "And I'm not glad about the fire. I'm only glad to get away from here." She remembered the arm, the clammy fingers holding her, the sucking, slurping sand.

Sam raised her eyebrows but didn't say anything. The truck rumbled to life, and soon, the flickering emergency lights were in the back mirror.

"What happened?" Sam said after a while of driving through the dark.

"The fire started in the kitchen." Cate shifted her legs. The farther they got from her house, the more her muscles tensed up. Maybe she'd been in shock after all. Not physically; it was only a little scratchy to breathe. But emotionally.

"What started it?" Sam glanced at her.

"I don't know."

"Don't worry about it," Helene's voice came from the narrow backseat. "Not tonight. We'll find out soon enough. There'll be an investigation."

"I suppose so." Cate's mind skipped back to the police officers that had come to her house. Wallis or Willis, and the tired woman who'd had too much coffee. "Yes. I suppose there will be an investigation." She pressed a hand to her chest to stifle a cough.

They were driving through the flats. The only light from a weak moon and their headlights, the beam revealing flashes of purple heather, green gorse, goldenrod.

Then they arrived, and Maisie and Ellie were waiting in the bright square of the door, and they had tea and macadamia cookies and lots of questions. Then there was the familiar peace of the Jack and Jill and the soft bed smelling of Maisie's dryer sheets, a call to Em, who was safe and not too scared, and finally, silence.

Only the sea hummed a lullaby to soothe her human sisters.

Chapter 25

Cate didn't sleep.

Instead, she watched the night and listened to the shadows. The longer she lay, the deeper seemed the dark. The longer she listened, the likelier seemed a scream, a yell, a choked warning outside her door.

Cate rolled her head from one side to the other, trying to relax her neck. The pillow was too high. Her jaw hurt.

Had she left on the flame under the kettle when she'd made tea? But even if... How had the flame jumped? Onto what?

Cate had no curtains in the kitchen. Her tea towels hung by the sink. The potholders were in a drawer. The roll of kitchen paper was of course flammable, but still so far away. If she'd really forgotten to switch off the stove, it seemed like only the kettle should've burned. Melted metal and a scorched cooktop should've been the extent of the damage.

Cate pushed the duvet down, then turned on her side, then scrunched the duvet into a roll and used it to support her leg. Her calf hurt. From knee to ankle her skin burned as if remembering the blistering run through the house. She should put something on it. Arnica gel, if Maisie had any. Gingerly, Cate touched her leg in the dark, but there was no wound or tenderness.

Maybe it'd been an electrical fire. Whatever that actually was. Cate pulled the duvet back up, imagining sparks jumping from the outlet by the pressure cooker. Sparks so hot, they ignited the countertop. It was a cheap plastic compound, not granite or quartz.

A bad time for a sabbatical, even though they had insurance. How much did Allen have in his account? A little? A lot?

Cate jerked upright. Allen!

He didn't know about the fire. She flicked on the light and rifled with shaking hands through her purse for the cell. She tapped his number.

No reply, only the automated response. Cate hit the call button again. Again, Allen didn't answer.

Where was he? He hadn't said. Nor when he was planning to come back.

There was a fire in the kitchen. A lot of damage to the house. We're okay.

Cate hesitated, then deleted the last sentence. *I'm at BCI*, she wrote instead. *Where are you? Please call.*

Gripping the phone, she got out of bed and padded barefoot into the bathroom that joined the Jack and Jill bedrooms. In the dim glow of a nightlight shaped like a sailboat—leave it to Maisie—she saw the door to Helene's room slightly gap open. Gently, Cate pushed against it.

Helene's sheets rustled. "Cate? Is that you?"

"Yes." Cate tiptoed over the cold floorboards to sit on her sister's bed.

Helene took her hand. "Cate." Her face was pale in the dim moonlight. "That fire was no accident. You've got to get out of that marriage."

Cate shook her head. A plastic counter could burn. Plastic burned.

"I told you." Helene gripped Cate's hand tighter. "I've seen it happen before."

Cate knew she should smile and explain no, there was no way, it had been the stove and the tea kettle. It was her fault.

But instead, Cate said nothing. Instead, she held on to her sister like a drowning person, unable to open her mouth. If she did, the quicksand might get her.

"Why don't you see it, Cate?" Helene's voice pleaded with her. "Why can't you connect the dots?"

"Because it's dangerous," Cate whispered suddenly. "Because it's so dangerous for me to connect the dots, Helene."

Helene dropped her hand, and for a moment, Cate thought her younger sister was angry again. But Helene got on her knees and reached for Cate, pulling her into an embrace that smelled of smoke and Maisie's shampoo and Ellie's cookies. "You're a woman with grown kids and a career, Cate, not a little girl who has to keep her head down to survive. It's dangerous *not* to connect the dots."

Cate's phone buzzed.

"What's that?" Helene rocked back.

"My cell." Cate grabbed it and checked the screen.

"It's Allen."

"Don't," Helene said. "Seriously, Cate. Don't answer him."

Cate exhaled sharply. "I can't have this hanging over my head. I can't do it any longer."

Helene sank back on her heels, her hands folded as if for prayer, the knuckles bright with pressure.

A memory flashed through Cate's mind.

She'd seen her sister sit like this before.

Helene was maybe six years old, the narrow childhood bed a vast plain between them. Cate cowered on the end, hugging her legs and pressing her cheek into her knees.

Mother hadn't talked to Cate for the third day in a row. Cate didn't know what she'd done wrong. She only knew she felt like drowning, and that Helene kept her from sinking altogether.

"Maybe if you do the dishes," Helene urged in a high whisper. "Maybe if you just do the dishes, she'll like you again."

"I did the dishes." Cold tears ran down Cate's leg, shimmied between shin and arm. "I already did everything."

"Maybe if you try harder?"

Cate nodded. She'd been lazy, it was true. She'd not put her shoes away, and she'd fed the bunny the good salad without thinking it through. From now on, Cate could never forget anything again. She could make no more mistakes. She had to try harder because she needed Mother to love her. If Mother could only love her, Cate would be safe.

Her cell phone buzzed again, pulling Cate back. Allen's face still flashed on the screen.

Helene was right. She was no longer a little girl, scared to death of stepping out of line.

Cate pressed the key. "Allen. Where are you?"

"I saw your text. What happened?"

"There was a fire in the kitchen."

"In the kitchen?"

"We think that's where it started. The firefighters will know more tomorrow." Cate rubbed her cigarette scar. "Where are you?"

"What happened? Tell me exactly."

Cate recounted the escape. "I don't know anything more. But—" Her voice hitched, and she cleared her throat. "I wonder, Allen. Was it an accident? I don't understand how the fire could've started."

She waited, holding her breath.

"Are you alone?" Allen asked.

Chapter 26

Cate uncurled and put her feet on the ground. The wood was cold, but it was solid.

"Yes." Cate nodded at Helene. "I'm alone, Allen. Talk to me."

"I need your help."

"What do you need?"

"I need you to help me," Allen repeated, and there was a trace of the old impatience in his voice. "Remember—you promised. For the marriage. And for the kids. Claire, especially."

"I remember. I need to know what's going on, Allen."

Helene nodded encouragement, and Cate felt a calm settle over her, as if she'd suddenly spotted a way to simply step out of the corner that had trapped her. "You need to tell me the truth." She lowered her voice. "Thank heaven the girls weren't home when it happened. But I'm done playing games."

This time, Allen answered at once. "The fire was no accident. That car outside the house?"

"Yes." Cate frowned. "What about it?"

"I'm pretty sure they were looking for me. I think

they set the fire. I was afraid something like this would happen."

Cate closed her eyes. The pieces of the puzzle shouldn't fit together. And yet they did. "Did you leave Beach Cove because you thought something might happen at the house?"

What about herself? And the *kids*? What if Em hadn't randomly called, or Cate would've turned over and fallen back asleep?

"Yes." He sounded oblivious. "That's why I left. I thought it'd be safer."

"Allen—" Cate didn't know what to say. He'd left to save himself, leaving his family exposed to danger.

And then Cate opened her eyes. Allen had stepped over her line in the sand a long time ago, but now she finally saw. This was it. This was the end.

She chose her words carefully. "Who are they? The men that set the fire. The men in the car."

"I mean, I don't know their names." His voice rose to the degree hers had dropped.

"You've got to give me more than that, Allen. What *do* you know?"

He breathed into the line. "It's the people from the shop window, Cate. They tracked me down."

He couldn't be serious. "You said you left them money." There had never been a shop window. Of course not. The question was, what had happened instead?

"I don't understand it either. I covered the cost. Maybe someone came along and stole the money before the owner could find it? Yes. That's probably what happened. And now they're hunting me down. I'm, uh, I'm kind of stuck where I am, Cate. I can't come back right now. But when the cops find out it was arson—"

When, not if.

"—there'll be an investigation. It would put the press on my trail. You know, ruin my career."

The police had come to talk to her. Men in cars had staked out the house. And Allen had lied so she'd give him a false alibi.

Cate turned her face away from the phone to exhale. When she spoke, she kept her voice as even as she could. "I see how it is. You don't want that to happen, of course. Listen, Allen, don't worry about me. I know what to do. I've got this."

"That's good. Our marriage is the most important thing to me. I want to work really hard on it."

"I want to work really hard on this too," Cate said. "So where are you?"

"Can I count on you?" Again, he didn't answer her question. Already, the sticky-sweet whine of manipulation was gone from his voice. Instead, a threat vibrated in his words.

"You can count on me," Cate said. Beside her, Helene moved nervously.

Cate's mind whirred. She couldn't ask again where Allen was. He wasn't going to answer and might grow angry. He'd already put them in danger once. What else was he capable of?

She needed time to think. She needed a plan.

"I hear someone," she said in a hushed tone,

warning Helene with a finger not to speak. "I have to go; I don't want anyone to overhear us."

"Good. Good idea, Cate. Keep all of this close to the chest."

"I'll see what I can learn from the fire inspector tomorrow," she continued. "See if the car comes back. I'll let you know. Call me at noon?" It would give her time to talk with the girls and decide what to do next. First of all, she needed to make sure Claire and Em were safe.

"Good plan. I can count on you, can't I? Don't mess this up, Cate."

Something squirmed in Cate's stomach. A wall broke, a membrane tore with a rip that felt audible. Anger came rushing in, flooding Cate and filling her belly, rising into her throat and squeezing her vocal cords into a whisper. "I won't mess up." She clenched a fist. "I promise. Stay in touch, Allen."

She heard him breathe into the line. Then he hung up.

Cate looked at Helene.

"Was it him? Did he start the fire?"

"No," Cate responded. "I don't think it was him. But he knows who did it, though he won't tell me. Something else entirely is happening."

There was a light knock on the door. It opened before the women could react, and Maisie's head appeared. "Oh." She looked at Helene and Cate, then softly entered on bare feet. "Sorry, Helene. I thought this was Cate's room. Are you two okay?" She pulled her fleece robe close and sat next to Cate on the bed.

"I don't know how to answer that," Cate said at the same time Helene said, "I don't know where to start," and then they heard steps in the hall.

"Ah," Maisie said. "There she is."

Ellie nudged the door wider, looking over her shoulder back in the hall. "Are you talking about me?"

"Always." Maisie scooched over on the bed. Helene pulled her legs higher to make space, and Ellie sat between them.

"What's going on?" Ellie asked. "Why are we sitting in the dark like roosting chickens?"

"Cate?" Helene leaned forward to see around Maisie and Ellie.

"It's about the fire," Cate started. "Or really, it's about Allen."

She paused and pressed a hand to her stomach. Not because it hurt, but because she felt empty. Not hungry, just empty. The fear that had filled her was gone. Cate lifted her chest and squared her shoulders, letting the unfamiliar void expand.

She knew time would fill it. Because she had daughters. She had a sister. And she had friends.

Cate inhaled into the new space and told the girls everything that had happened. The tinted car, the visit from the officers, her false alibi, Allen's last call.

Helene leaned against the headboard, hugging the cover draped over her knees. Maisie and Ellie sat in silence.

"It doesn't make sense. The men in the car were watching your house before Allen came up with his window story." There was no judgment for Cate in

Ellie's voice.

"Yes." Cate shook her head. "There are so many things I didn't put together."

"No wonder." Helene's voice came from the far side of the bed. "Even now, we're barely scratching the surface."

Maisie put an arm around Cate. "You stay here, Cate. Claire too; the Jack and Jill are perfect for you. There'll be no men in cars watching Beach House. I promise."

Cate smiled. "How can you be so sure?"

"There's no casual parking on Seashore Lane. They won't blend into the beach heather. And I'm going to ask Vince to keep an eye out," Maisie declared. "Something tells me he's good at that sort of thing."

Ellie hummed her agreement. "What do you want to do next, Cate?"

"I think... I'll go back to the house."

She felt Ellie and Maisie exchanging glances. Helene crinkled her sheets.

"I'm not going to pretend I can fix this anymore," Cate promised. "That's over. But I want to see what I can find out. Allen keeps everything. There must be documents in his files showing what he's been up to; plane tickets, restaurant bills, that sort of thing. Maybe I can piece together what's happening."

"Uh," Ellie said, sounding alarmed. "That sounds extremely unsafe, Cate. They've tried to burn down your house—with you *in it*. I'd much rather you don't go back."

"Don't go back, Cate," Helene echoed.

"Just once," Cate said. "Or twice. See what I can find."

"I'll come with you," Maisie said suddenly. "Ells, you come too. And Sam. There's safety in numbers."

Ellie moaned. "I *hate* death by fire."

"My plane leaves tomorrow." Helene also sounded unhappy. "Should I delay? I want to help too."

Cate bent backward to see her sister. "Don't change the ticket," she said. "I never meant to pull you into any of this. Besides, you've helped more than enough."

"Come stay with me or send the girls. I'll keep them safe," Helene promised. She reached around Ellie and Maisie; Cate did the same, and for a moment, their fingertips touched.

"As a last resort," Cate said. "I don't want to upset their routines any more than necessary. But I'm sure they'd love to visit when this is over."

"It's late." Maisie stood, pulling Ellie with her. "Don't talk too long, you two. We can talk tomorrow." On her way out, she murmured, "I'll just make a quick call," and Cate knew she meant Vince. Ellie closed the door behind them, and their footsteps faded.

Cate too got off the bed. For a moment, she looked out of the window. The new moon had risen over the clouds.

So much had changed since Helene had stepped out of the fog. Cate didn't have a house or a husband anymore. She smiled. "We've made progress, Helene. Haven't we?"

Helene slid under her cover, blond hair spilling

over the pillow in a familiar pattern. "I think we both still have a long way to go."

"It doesn't have to be short. It just has to be in the right direction."

"Good night, Cate."

"Good night, Helene."

Chapter 27

Sam narrowed her eyes at the dark. She'd been fast asleep a moment before, but not anymore. Now, she felt like it was high noon. Earlier, even. Eleven. Eleven in the morning, the most awake time there was.

The fire hadn't been an accident. She should've told Cate. Cate needed to be careful.

Something rustled in the shadows.

Sam sat up, holding her breath. No—nothing. Maybe an opossum had snarled in the yard, or a wave had crashed onto the beach.

The alarm clock showed three in the morning. Her personal witching hour. Sam often woke up at three, and rarely could she find a reason for it.

She lay for a while longer, trying to fall back asleep, listening to the ocean's faint white noise. Then she groaned and tossed off her cover. "Fine."

Sam slipped her feet into the fluffy slippers that looked cute with her secret babydoll nightie—so secret, not even Larry knew about it—and shuffled to the desk in the corner. Charging her phone there instead of the nightstand was the latest attempt at squelching a mild screen addiction.

She tapped Larry's name on the screen. She'd given him plenty of time; he should've called her fifteen times over. Not even a text. That's what she'd gotten.

"Sam. Why are you calling? Did you—" Larry sounded nervous, or maybe angry, but he stopped.

Sam heard him inhale. She stepped to the window to look for the opossum. "Did I...what?" What had he meant to ask?

Larry's voice was nicer when he spoke again. Less edgy. "Isn't it really late in Beach Cove? Are you okay?"

"I am, but I'm seriously starting to wonder whether you are," Sam said. "You didn't call me back as promised." Sam couldn't remember if Larry had actually promised, but it didn't matter. The promise should've been implied. "I don't know where you are, or with whom, or what you're doing. I'm worried."

"I called you!" Larry sounded genuinely surprised. "We talked."

"No, Larry, you didn't call me." Exasperation crept into Sam's voice. "*I* called *you*, and you said you couldn't talk because you had to go to dinner."

"I think you've got it wrong. I swear *I* called *you*. I told you I'm with Patrick."

Sam knew Larry wasn't lying. He'd paid so little attention, the facts had gotten twiddled in his brain.

"So you're good?" she asked curtly. He was alive. She'd gotten her answer. She wasn't going to stand here in babydoll and mussed hair, phoning after her husband like a '50s Stepford wife. She had her own life to live, or at least a warm bed to get back to. Watching

TV would lift her mood more than arguing with Larry.

"Working," Larry said, unaware of her anger. "Always working. The manuscripts are fascinating."

"Yeah?" Golden Girls sometimes ran late at night.

"There's more to do than I thought." He paused.

Sam smirked. There was always more to do for Larry. Working on his relationship, for example, though that one never seemed to make the list.

"Okay." She fished for the TV remote, weighing it in her hand. It was too light. She'd forgotten to put new batteries in, so now she had to go in the basement to find the box. "Anything else, Larry?"

"Did you..." He paused, which made Sam look up.

"What?"

Larry coughed. "Nothing, just a tickle in the throat. Uh. What's going on with you, Sam? What's happening in Beach Cove?"

"What's happening in Beach Cove? Cate's house caught fire."

"Ha."

"No, really. She woke up to a house fire. She barely got her sister out."

"Are you serious? Are they okay?"

"Yes and yes. They're at the inn."

"What happened? Was it the dryer?"

"I don't know. Frankly, I don't have a good feeling."

"About what?"

"The cause of the fire. Keep up, Lar."

"Right. Well, tell Cate good luck, and whatever we can do to help. Keep me posted, okay?"

Sam smiled. "Will do."

"Anything else?" He sounded leery of more Beach Cove news.

"Nothing else. Oh, wait." There was something. "Bonnie came to the store."

"Uh-oh." Larry coughed. "What did she want?"

"She asked about you."

"She asked about *me*? Why, Sam?"

"Who knows? But she asked where you are. And what it is you do."

When Larry spoke again, Sam could practically hear his frown. "Did she tell you why she needs to know that?"

Sam tilted her head. "I figure it's because you told every soul in town what an important historian you are. You've made people curious." In fact, Sam wasn't sure at all academic interest had brought Bonnie to the store. But trying to guess the woman's motives was labor lost and curiosity as good an explanation as any.

"It's none of her business. I don't trust the woman. Sam, don't tell Bonnie anything about me. Just tell her you don't know."

"Okay." Sam raised her eyebrows. Bonnie freaked her out too, but why Larry? He wasn't even in Beach Cove. What did he care about how much a beautiful fisherwoman knew?

"What does she already know?"

"About what?"

Larry grunted impatiently. "About me. What I do, where I am."

"Uh." Sam tried to think. "She knows you're

working with Syrian manuscripts, and that you're doing it at the Turkish coast."

Larry hissed. "How does she know that? I never told her *anything*. I never even talked with Sagartati. She's too weird. I don't like her. Don't tell her about me, Sam. Talk about something else when you meet her."

Sam felt her eyebrows travel into her hairline. "She's a *bit* weird, Larry, calm down. I'm telling her as little as I can without being rude. No need to yell."

"I'm not..." Larry took a raspy breath. "I'm not yelling."

"Let's not waste our time talking about Bonnie," Sam said tactfully. Who knew her husband was so scared of the woman? Sam couldn't remember the two ever meeting, though of course there was plenty going on in Beach Cove she didn't know about.

"I've got to go, Sam. Do me a favor and stay away from Bonnie. I don't think she's a good influence on you."

"Larry, I'm not your teenage daughter. Don't worry about my influences."

"Just...just...fine." Larry sighed, sounding resigned. "Call me if something happens, Sam."

"Or if I just want to talk?"

"I have to work."

It was like a punch in the chest. A small one, because Sam had heard it before. Never from half the world away, though. "How about you just buy yourself a newspaper," she snapped. "I'm not going to call again if you can't be bothered to talk."

Larry groaned. "I'm sorry. I love you, Sammy. I do."

"Then why doesn't it feel like it?"

"Sam—"

But Sam ended the call before Larry could finish.

She tossed the phone back on the desk and went to sit on the bed, hugging a pillow.

Was love supposed to be this complicated? Was marriage supposed to feel this lonely?

Chapter 28

Maisie and Ellie occupied the patio chairs on either side of Cate, framing her like sentinels.

Helene sat opposite, her hands resting on her lap, her eyes shielded by glamorous sunglasses. Between them, the table was loaded with a coffee carafe, tea, a basket with croissants, jam, cheese, yogurt. Despite the early hour, Ellie had opened the umbrella to shade the table from the rising sun. None of them were eating, and the only sound came from the water in the cove, the gulls and the sandpipers.

"I don't think you should go back after all, Cate," Maisie said. She shuffled her empty coffee cup to the other side of her plate, then back. "Stay here where it's safe. With us."

"They said it'd be okay for me to go in as long as I stay out of the kitchen and don't go upstairs. There's plenty of damage, but nothing's going to collapse."

"You do have insurance?" Ellie wanted to know.

"Yes. All the documents are in a fire safe."

"It's not falling debris I'm worried about," Maisie said darkly.

"If you're not coming with me, I think you should

go back and see what you can find out," Helene said. "Cate needs to sort this out."

"You want her to be safe, don't you?" Maisie countered. "They said it was arson. A crime has been committed. Who knows what they'll try next?"

Helene slid her shades lower, gazing over the brim. "The danger isn't at the house right now; it's a public spectacle over there. There'll be angry neighbors monitoring the street very closely. I bet they're as ready as breeding ospreys to attack anyone who acts suspicious."

Maisie frowned but didn't respond.

Helene sighed. "There's probably a cop taking photographs of spectators right now. If the arsonist has even the intelligence of an eggplant, he'll stay away." She stood. "Somehow, Cate has to get to the bottom of this. I agree with her that the real danger would be not going back."

"They stopped the fire before it reached the hallway," Cate said. "The computer is in the bedroom, so it should be fine. I'll grab our papers, Allen's files and the hard drive. We'll hook it up here and then all I need is Allen's password to get in."

"He's told you what it is?" Helene's eyebrows lifted with surprise.

"Of course he hasn't. But some keys on the keyboard are more worn than others, and I'm good at word jumbles." In fact, she was pretty certain his password was the company name followed by the numbers one, two, three. Allen wasn't as smart as he thought.

"I like word puzzles too," Ellie said. "I'm in. Maisie, come on. Don't backpaddle."

"Oh, fine. They'll not gun all of us down at once, I suppose." Chairs scraped over pavers as they got up. "But we're coming straight back," Maisie added firmly. "It's a visit to collect evidence. That's it. You're not staying in Allen's house. You'll stay here."

"Move in for good," Ellie said. "Sell your house instead of fixing it. Live with us, Cate."

"Yes." Maisie took Cate's hands. "Beach House has more than enough space for you and Claire."

Cate could see her friends were serious; she heard it in their voices. Even Helene was nodding approval; like Ellie, Cate and Claire could live here.

Maisie had mentioned staying at Beach House the night before, but Cate had assumed it was only until she'd rebuild. But now she realized she'd never fix her house. She wanted to tear it down because the place had been a trap, not a home.

Yet her knee-jerk instinct was no, of course she couldn't accept the offer. She couldn't simply move into her friends' house and inconvenience them, could she?

"I did," Ellie said as if she'd read Cate's thoughts. "I live here now, and it's lovely."

"The more, the merrier," Maisie agreed. "I was lonely on my own. Now even Ellie starts to bore me."

Ellie grinned. "It's not true, I'm super entertaining," she said. "But do move in, Cate. Claire too. We need some young blood to keep us on our toes."

"I...uh." Cate hesitated. It sounded too good to be true.

"I'd sleep a lot easier at night if you'd move in with them," Helene said. She took off the sunglasses. "And Beach House is much nicer than your own. Don't be stupid now."

Cate inhaled the sea air, then exhaled and let go. Her old life was over now. The next one would be her own, and she'd live it on her terms. "Thank you, Maisie, Ellie," she said. "I'd love to move in. If you're sure."

"We're sure," Ellie said without a moment's hesitation. "We've been sure for a while."

Maisie clapped her hands. "We really hoped we could talk you into it, Cate. It's so obvious, isn't it? Come on all, let's sit down again. Let's have our first breakfast together before we go to Cate's house. Or Allen's, more like. It always had too much Allen in it, and I'm glad it's gone."

Gratefulness filled Cate, rising warm from her belly to her cheeks. Even her fingertips prickled.

She was about to sit back down when Helene's phone vibrated. Helene checked it, then walked over to Cate and pulled her into a hug. "I'm glad you'll live with them," she whispered into Cate's ear. "I'd hate to lose you now that I've finally found you."

"I'll be okay," Cate promised and hugged Helene back. "Who called you?"

Helene stepped back. "The Sandpiper Inn sent a car, and it's waiting out front. I've got to get to the airport."

"Today?" They still had so much to talk about.

"Something came up. I have to go back." Helene studied the diamond on her finger, then let her hand drop by her side and pinched her lips into a vague line. "Can't be helped."

"Bad?"

Helene had never hinted at being anything but successful. But she was only human, with many failures bolstering each achievement.

"Not sure." Helene gave a tight shrug.

"If it is, come back," Cate said. "You've always got me."

"Okay," Helene smiled. "Thank you, Cate. For talking when it was difficult. And for saving my life last night."

"Thank you for coming. I know you were angry. I'm glad you didn't give up on me."

"No." Helene lifted her Birkin from the back of the chair. "At least I never did that."

Helene nodded goodbye at Maisie and Ells. "Watch her closely," she instructed. "She's a recovering addict."

Ellie shook her curls back. "No, she isn't. She's not addicted to abuse. It's just hard to get out, that's all. But Cate's got this."

Helene smiled at Ellie. "Good." She bumped lightly into Cate on her way out, resting her head on Cate's shoulder for a moment. "Eat something, kid," she murmured. "I hate to see you waste away."

"Call me."

Helene nodded, walked down the patio steps and

left through the gate.

"Am I interrupting?"

They turned around. William stood in the door of the sunroom.

Of course Cate knew about the inn's guest, but they hadn't met yet. Too much had happened. But she liked the way he looked. Friendly and professional.

"You're not interrupting at all," Maisie replied kindly. "Did you and Vince find any mice in the basement this morning?"

"They check the traps every morning and night because they catch so many," Ellie whispered. "I'll never ever *ever* set foot in that basement."

"No, not today." Vince appeared behind William, lifting an empty trap as proof.

Where William was short, Vince was tall, and where William was soft, Vince was not. But Cate saw similarities in the way they moved and talked.

"We're trying out new traps. Best to give it a bit and not to disturb anything downstairs," Vince said.

"Of course not." Maisie glanced at Ellie. "Come on, you two. Sit down. We're about to have breakfast." The men came willingly, Vince depositing his trap out of sight behind the wall and William bringing one more chair.

Ellie scanned the table. "I'll get another plate."

"No." Cate pointed at her own, unused setting. "I want to get to the house before anyone else does." Allen in particular. If one of them was going to snatch the computer, it'd be her.

"Oh but..." Maisie pursed her mouth. "What about

celebrating moving in with us?"

Vince leaned forward. "Another friend moving in?"

"Yes!" Maisie beamed. "We got Cate."

Cate tensed, expecting irritation to show in Vince's face. Surely, he wanted to catch Maisie on her own as much as possible, not have all her friends hang around.

But he looked at Cate with satisfaction. "Congratulations. Now we're neighbors too."

Cate felt her face heat up. She didn't know what to say. Vince had always intimidated her. But then she reminded herself that all that was over. She didn't have to be scared of anyone any longer. "Thank you," she said. And louder, "I'm grateful they're having me."

"Of course they are," Vince said, and William smiled as if he were in on a little joke. "They've been plotting how to get you for a while."

"How do you even..." Maisie raised an eyebrow. "*Plotting* is a strong word, isn't it?"

Vince took a croissant. "My apologies. In my defense, I rather like when you're busy plotting something, and I'm glad to see it work out."

Now it was Maisie's turn to blush. Cate smiled. "You stay and entertain your guests," she told Ellie and Maisie. "I'm going to the house with Sam. She's probably in the village already."

Ellie looked disappointed, but then William poured coffee into her cup and winked at her. "Uh, okay," she said, frowning at her guest. "We'll help pack your things this afternoon, though. Okay?"

"Yes," Maisie said. Her color was back to normal. "How about furniture?"

"I have no idea what to do, Maisie. I'll have to find out how it works."

"The divorce? Find out how the divorce works?" Ellie jumped in.

Cate couldn't speak, but she nodded.

"Well, I can tell you all about it," Ellie said dryly. "Be ready to fight for each chair and sofa cushion."

"I don't want them," burst from Cate. She put a hand over her mouth, surprised. Then she dropped it again. "I don't want anything from that house. Just my books and photos and the kids' things. Allen won't fight me over any of it. He can have everything else."

"No, don't let him win this easily," Ellie warned. "Get your share. You can start a nest egg for the kids."

"First things first. Right now, I want the computer and files."

"That's exactly right," Maisie said. "We can do the rest later. Who knows what even survived the fire? There'll be smoke damage too, you know. You'll figure it out; you've always been the smart one."

"I wish." Cate waved and walked into the house to get her purse.

Vince came after her. "You'll need a lift. May I drive you?"

"Oh." Cate wasn't used to having men consider her needs. She'd forgotten that her car wasn't waiting outside. It was still at her house.

"Maisie will have my head if you say no," Vince added politely.

"Okay," Cate said shyly. "Thank you. I can drive myself back, so you won't have to wait."

"Not a problem." Vince closed the patio door behind him and walked Cate to the front door, expertly opening it before she could reach for the handle. "To be honest, I'm quite curious about what happened," he said casually, unlocking Maisie's Acura.

Cate clambered in, feeling awkward but also spoiled by his chivalry. "Me too," she said. "I'm curious, too."

Vince got into the driver's seat and backed into the road, and as they drove back to the scene of the crime, Cate told him everything she remembered about the fire.

Chapter 29

Sam flipped the sign in the door to *Closed*, stuck a post-it note below that read 'due to personal circumstances,' and locked the bookstore. Cate had called; she was at her house. With Vince.

Of all people.

Usually, Vince was in Maisie's basement.

Personally, Sam had never come across mouse traps that needed so much attention. But that was just her and her own traps.

At least her gut stayed quiet when she thought of all the mice and men practically living in the inn's cellar. And Maisie had promised to keep an eye on the situation.

Though maybe, just as a precaution, Sam would stop by the local pet store. See if they'd had any large orders for mice lately.

She rummaged in her bag for the key to the truck when a flash of red caught her eye.

"Bonnie?" Sam froze, shocked to see the fisherwoman step out of the Candy Apple Store. In her hand she carried a pink paper bag with a green ribbon.

Not only was it the second time Bonnie had come

into the village—normally, weeks or months passed between encounters—but Sam had never seen Bonnie eat candy. Or apples. Or, come to think of it, anything at all.

"Sam." Bonnie lifted her head like a pointer smelling a rabbit.

For once, she wasn't dressed in salt-and-oil-stained rags. Instead she wore jeans and a knit sweater. Both clean, both fitted, and both, Sam recognized, from a cheap mega-store. But on Bonnie, they looked like tailored designer wear.

"Where is Larry?" Bonnie asked, her voice flat like the sea on a quiet day.

Sam rubbed her arm. Her skin prickled; the little hairs rose. For sure the woman had been raised by a pack of wolves. Or sharks. What did she want from Larry?

Sam considered a snarky response, but the fisherwoman's green eyes seemed to flash a warning, and she swallowed the snark back down. Better to keep things nice and normal. With Bonnie, even the pretense of normal was good.

"He's good," Sam said, as breezy as she could make it. "Doing his thing, you know?" At once, she regretted the question mark inflection. She didn't want to talk about Larry. "So how are *you*? Buying candy apples? Do you like them?" She felt hot. Babbling wasn't her strong suit.

"No." Bonnie lifted the pink bag, frowning at it.

"Okay." The small bag clearly showed the outline of a large chocolate apple. Sam had sampled enough of them to recognize the uneven surface caused by marshmallows in the coating. Rocky Road apple. "Uh...is this for someone else?" Bonnie wasn't going to bury the apple and dance around her sacrifice, after all.

"It's for—" Bonnie seemed to consider. "It's for Brandie."

Sam felt her eyebrows rise as if they were attached to strings. Left field again. "Your *daughter* Brandie?" Bonnie's daughter had left Beach Cove soon after Alex had disappeared.

"Yes."

"I'm so..." Sam paused, embarrassed at her sluggish mental reflexes. Happy? Glad? Was that the correct sentiment? After all, they'd never found out for sure why Brandie had left. They'd assumed it was to avoid the suspicion automatically cast on whoever was last with a missing person. Even if it was a sixteen-year-old girl.

"She's back now." Bonnie let the bag sink again. "And she remembered the chocolate apples."

It was the single most human thing Sam had ever heard Bonnie say. She blinked, touched. The poor girl, being ripped from her mom like that. "Of course. I'm so..." Again she struggled for words. "Bonnie, I'm so glad she's back," Sam said in the end, and she meant it. "I never knew exactly why she left. Was it because of Alex?"

Bonnie's face was a deep pool. "Alex. The son of your friend Maisie."

Sam tilted her head. If she didn't know Bonnie

was highly intelligent in her own way, she'd think the woman couldn't understand English. "Yes. Alex and Brandie were dating back then."

Bonnie's eyes suddenly caught the light, glinting as if she was laughing inside. "Yes, that's why Brandie left. People talked, and it annoyed her. She was young."

It was a surprisingly dispassionate way for a mother to put it, Sam thought. But Bonnie wasn't the type to air her personal business in front of strangers. Who knew her struggles? "Of course," Sam replied politely. "Well, say hi to your kid, Bonnie; I'm happy she's back. Uh. I have to get going. Cate's waiting for me."

"Ah, Cate." Something like satisfaction showed in the lift of Bonnie's lips. "There was a fire at her house."

"Yes." By now, the news had naturally spread through the community. "But she's okay, and so is her sister. Her sister was staying with her."

"Her daughters weren't."

Sam wanted to shake her head clear, just because every other sentence Bonnie said hit out of the blue. "Yes, luckily. How...um, how did you know?"

For a moment, Bonnie looked at her without answering, and Sam felt like she was being judged. Then the sea-lettuce eyes let her go. "Brandie," Bonnie said simply. "She texted Emily, Cate's eldest."

Anyone connected to Bonnie using something as normal as a cell phone was, in and of itself, not normal. "Sure," Sam said, trying not to draw the vowel out. "That makes sense."

Again the laughing light flashed in Bonnie's eyes. "Yes," she said. "It does, Sam." Without another word, she turned and walked away, her stride too long for the streets of the village. A spear or harpoon would've fitted Bonnie's gait better than the dangling pink paper bag.

"Okay. Good," Sam whispered. "Good. Good."

Would she see more of Bonnie now her daughter was back? Presumably, a twenty-six-year-old would be bored sitting in her mother's trailer on the cliff all day. Already, the girl was reaching out to her old friends. Friend. Em.

Sam went to her truck. What would Cate make of the friendship?

She drove lost in thought and a few minutes later, pulled up in front of Cate's burned house. "Goodness," Sam muttered under her breath, peering at the ruin. She was used to the house being neat and unremarkable. The lawn was torn up and there was a gaping black hole instead of the window Cate had looked out of when doing dishes. Tendrils of soot snaked up the vinyl siding like tentacles.

Sam was eyeing Maisie's white Acura, which was parked at an interesting angle, when the front door opened. She jumped out of the truck.

"Vince?" So far, he hadn't complained about the use of his first name. On the contrary, he'd joined the game.

"Hello, Sam," he replied and waved.

"Is Cate here?" Sam asked, explicitly not asking what *he* was doing here. Had things progressed to the point where he was dropping off Maisie's friends for her?

"She's inside, waiting for you. Me, she sent away." He pointed at the ruin. "You don't happen to know who did this, do you?"

The words were so casual, Sam didn't realize for a second how strange they were. "Of course not," she replied, taken aback. "I mean, it wasn't me. Do *you* know anything?"

He laughed as if she'd made a joke. "No, I don't either. Well, best not to linger. Goodbye." He hunched his shoulder and bowed his head in a greeting, then stalked off and folded himself into the white sedan.

This was the second time someone had laughed at Sam and left her standing.

"All right," Sam muttered. "I guess I'll *linger* by myself then." Shaking her head, she made her way over tire-marked grass and trampled daisies into the house.

Outside it smelled of stale smoke. Being inside was like walking into a fire pit.

Ash and soot motes floated in the air. The apricot walls had turned a dull gray with dark whiplash marks, matting to charcoal black near the kitchen. The fire had gnawed away the door and clawed at the jamb. The kitchen itself was a skeleton of beams and charred four-by-fours, dotted with remnants of singed drywall and melted vinyl, wet appliances and grimy glass shards.

Sam pursed her lips and exhaled, trying to process the violence. She wanted to walk away, get outside, back into the air and the sun. The front-yard daisies were crushed, but they were still daisies, not a black-toothed monster. "Stop it," she muttered. Her mind was trying to curl into the fetal position.

Because this had been no accident. Even if the fire marshal wouldn't have told them, she knew in her gut this was arson. This had been an attempt at—killing Cate?

Her gut lurched. Maybe?

No. No, that didn't feel right.

Sam rubbed her tongue against the roof of her mouth. The air tasted of smog and charred plastic. She took a few steps, trying to stay clear of debris. "Cate? Are you in here?"

"In the bedroom, Sam."

Cate sounded different. Busy. And firm. Sam turned toward the master bedroom. It had been spared from the fire and felt a little safer. "Hi. You okay?"

Cate was sitting on the ground, pulling plugs from outlets. The computer stood tucked under the desk, dry and protected. "I'm going to take it with me," Cate declared. "It works perfectly fine. I figured out Allen's password."

Sam looked over her shoulder. "Where is he?" Allen was unpleasant at the best of times. She didn't want to face him while hauling off his computer.

"I don't know." Cate pushed a strand of hair out of her eyes. Her face had thinned over the last weeks, and there was a smudge on her cheek. "He won't tell me." She looked at Sam. "He did admit last night he was afraid something would happen at the house. That's why he left."

Sam felt her jaw drop. "And he didn't warn you?"

"No. He didn't warn the *girls*." Cate stood and hauled the desktop into her arms. "Grab the monitor, Sam. I don't know if Maisie has a spare."

Sam did as she was told. "Goodness, Cate. I'm sorry. What a horrible thing for him to do."

Cate grabbed a stack of folders on her way out. "If Em wouldn't have called to ask about the Tylenol, Helene and I could've suffocated in our sleep. It was sheer dumb luck."

Again Sam thought it was more than an accident. Claire never had headaches. And Em *knew* Claire could take Tylenol. Even Sam knew Claire could take Tylenol because she forever got hurt playing sports.

Cate continued as they crossed the lawn, unaware of Sam's thoughts. "If Claire would've been home... Allen had no way of knowing, Sam." She pushed the computer into the backseat of the truck. "It didn't even occur to him to ask how we were. Like it was no big deal we just woke up in a burning house."

"You gotta get out, Cate. You know that, don't you?" Sam put the monitor on the backseat floor and followed Cate back into the house.

"Oh, I'm out." Cate seized a small suitcase and hitched a bag filled with books over her shoulder. She nudged her chin in the direction of a stack of paper-filled drawers on the desk. "Can you manage those? I just need to get my bathroom things, and then we can leave."

Sam shuffled the drawers into her arms. "You're *out*? Yes? It's finally over?"

"I'm out. But it's not over," came the dark response.

The corners of Sam's mouth dropped in respect. Yes, something had definitely changed in Cate. She was spitting-mad angry. And Cate was never angry. "Do let me know what I can do to help," Sam said and followed Cate back to the truck.

They stowed away Cate and Claire's belongings until the cab smelled like an old ashtray. Then they got in themselves, and Sam put the truck in gear.

"Are you going to be like this from now on?" she asked, checking traffic over her shoulder as she pulled into the road.

"Like how?"

"Angry? And mad?"

"Maybe for a while." Cate turned to catch a last glimpse of the house. "Until I'm divorced. Until I settle the score. Whichever comes first."

Sam drove for a while, adjusting to this new Cate. "Good for you, girl," she finally said. "About time you flipped the switch."

"I know." Cate rolled the window down. "To be honest, I've known for years."

"Good thing Helene came," Sam remarked after another pause, wondering whether she was pushing it. She still expected Cate to retreat the way she usually did. "And good thing there was a fire, and good thing nobody got hurt." Sam parked in Maisie's driveway.

Cate grinned, and Sam wondered if she'd ever seen Cate grin before.

"That's one way of looking at it," Cate said and let herself out.

Sam followed, taking the computer with her. "You have insurance on the house, don't you?"

"Yes," Cate said and pulled the suitcase out of the boot. "But guess what. I'm not rebuilding anything. For once, I'm simply getting rid of it." She rested the suitcase on the gravel, just shy of the steps leading to the red door, and looked up the big, old mansion. "The house can be razed to the ground for all I care. Claire and I are moving into Beach House."

As if on cue, the door opened, and Maisie and Ellie, Claire and Em, Vince, Tom, and even William came streaming out, some calling greetings and some hugging Cate, and all pulling bags from the truck.

Maisie came to stand by Sam, clutching a smoky stack of papers.

"Did Cate just say she's going to live here with you? Like, for good?" Sam asked.

Maisie hummed a yes. "You're next, Sam."

Sam blinked. "No. No way. I'm not moving. Thank you very much, and I love you, but that'd be a little too close for comfort. I need space."

Maisie was watching Cate, who was hugging both Claire and Em, suitcase forgotten. "If there's one thing Beach House has, it's space," she said. "So I guess we'll see, Sam, old friend." She chuckled and went into the house.

Sam looked after her.

It was the third time it'd happened.

Maybe it was just one of those days when things went a bit wonky and none of it meant anything. Because cross your heart and spit twice...

"It doesn't mean anything," Sam whispered to herself and lugged the computer higher in her arms. "It's fine. All normal." Softly, she followed her friends into Beach House and gently pushed the red door closed with her foot.

Chapter 30

"Ellie? Are you in here?"

In the backroom of the store, Ellie froze. Her fish knife hovered mid-air over the cutting board.

When the door had opened with that telltale swoosh of escaping air, she'd immediately thought of Gordy. He and she still had unfinished business. They'd taken a step that had awakened Ellie's curiosity, and maybe she wouldn't mind taking another step.

But the male voice out there didn't belong to Gordy. It belonged to—

"Ellilie? Hey. It's me. Are you in the back?"

Ellie's hand came down with enough force to drive the knife tip into the wood. "*Dale*?" When she let go of the handle, her hand shook. She wiped it on her checkered apron and strode to the door.

There he stood, her ex-husband. Black hair moussed, hands in the pockets of stylish jeans, sheepish little-boy expression on his face.

"Dale," Ellie repeated in a daze. Seeing him was like Magic Eraser for her mind, wiping out the smarts. She couldn't think. "What are you doing here?"

"I came to see you," Dale said and took his hands out of his pockets. For once, he wasn't making a show about the smell of fish in the store.

Two more Fish Market days. Only two more before Tom and Em took over, and here Dale walked into the store.

Ellie stepped back until she hit the backdoor. "You came to see me," she repeated stupidly.

Maybe it was the doorjamb smacking her head, or maybe her brain had reignited the pilot light all by itself. Suddenly, Ellie remembered that she was mad. And done. She was so done with Dale.

"Here I am." He looked at her expectantly.

"I'm sorry, what?" Ellie finally said.

"What?" Dale's expectant look turned confused. He ran a hand through his hair.

She used to love that hair. Of course. He'd always been attractive. "Dale." Ellie crossed her arms. "What are you doing here? Why are you—why are you *here*?"

"Right." He buried his hand back in his pocket and rocked back on his heels. "I miss you, Ellie. I know I've been a... I had it all wrong."

"You had it all wrong."

He looked to the floor, then peeked up with a little smile. But the boy routine didn't work on her anymore.

"Maybe you meant to go see Bonnie?" Ellie was unable to keep the frost out of her voice. "Maybe you're missing *her*."

"No." The coy smile slipped away. "That's what I got all wrong, Ellie."

"Is that right?" There was plenty more he'd gotten wrong; his passion for Bonnie was only the tip of an iceberg. Ellie pumped air into her lungs. "I thought it might've been leaving me without a warning or a chance to contact you. Or maybe, Dale, it was the fact that you sold our house out from under my son and me."

When he spoke, it was in his be-reasonable voice. "But I gave you the store, Ellie. You *love* the store." He rocked forward again.

"As a matter of fact, I don't love the store. But I wasn't done talking. Dale, the worst thing you did was leaving Tom."

"I told him I'd get in touch!"

"You said—no, you *wrote* him—that you'd get in touch when you were ready."

Dale nodded. "Yes. I just needed some space. And time."

"You're a parent, Dale. Tommy relied on you to be there for him, always. You don't get to be conditional."

"Oh, come on." Dale shrugged as if it was a bad joke. "Everyone gets a little time off now and then. For mental health?"

Ellie bit the inside corner of her mouth and turned to the window so she wouldn't have to look at her ex.

It was lovely outside. A last rearing of sun and heat before the leaves started to fall and the summer was over. What had she done to deserve Dale coming back to spoil it all?

"So I'll talk with him. It'll be okay, Ellie. Tom's grown, and he's a laid-back guy."

"Tom's *angry*."

Dale's eyebrows dropped, and his Adam's apple jumped as he swallowed words.

"You didn't miss me, Dale," Ellie said. "And you can't come back to pick up where you left off. Is that what you meant to do?"

"I messed up. I know, Ells."

"Then why don't you leave, Dale? Go back where you came from."

"We should talk, Ellie. I know I've hurt your feelings. I was really confused."

"Don't I know it." Ellie shook her head. "The damage you caused in your confusion is permanent. I have a new life. You're not in it."

"It's not that easy, Ellie," Dale said. "Because I'm back. I'm back in Beach Cove, and if your new life is here, I'll be in it."

Ellie closed her eyes. "No. You can't come back. You don't even like Beach Cove."

"Everybody likes Beach Cove. It's cute."

Ellie opened one eye to glare at her ex. The man had no connection at all to the place. Only tourists thought Beach Cove was *cute*.

It was true the town sweetly wore its cobbled streets and quaint stores. But there was more to the place, something real and raw that slumbered in the beaches and the waves, the way friends stuck together, the fogs and dark cliffs, the unlikely blue of the cove.

"Are you serious?" Ellie opened her other eye. "You're moving back here? Do you have a place?"

"Not yet. But Carl is going to work in Europe for a few months. I could rent his house and probably get my old job back. And... yes, I was hoping to get my old life back. With you and Tom in it."

"Don't." Ellie's stomach tilted like a drunk sailor. She couldn't deal with Dale again. She wanted her new beginning, her inn and her son.

She wanted the clean slate she'd been promised.

Dale's face changed as if a mask slipped off. His eyes widened, and his winsome smile shortened; even his hair seemed to change from moussed to messy. "I miss you, Ellie. I miss Tom, too. I miss... I miss having a family."

"Oh no." Ellie let her head roll back into her neck. "Don't do this, please. *You* left *us*. You abandoned us. You betrayed me and our marriage and wrote letters to Bonnie. There's no family left. There's no us. I don't want it."

"Let me show you how much I've changed, Ellie."

Ellie felt the knot of anger inside her slip loose. Should she talk with Dale, work through her anger and make him understand how much he'd let them down? She didn't know.

"Please let me take you out for dinner. Just once. Just one chance to talk."

Ellie weaved her head from side to side. "If we have dinner, and I'm not saying we do." She paused. "But if we did, will you leave Beach Cove afterward?"

Dale's eyes fixed on her as if she were a rabbit. "I want a fair chance to explain and tell you how much I miss you. If you still want me to leave after that, I'll go.

I'd do anything for you."

Ellie's head weave turned into a proper shake. She didn't believe his promise. She'd been married for too long to the man; she knew him too well. He wasn't simply going to go away if he wanted something.

One way or the other, she had to talk with Dale. Make him see his cause was hopeless.

"Fine," she said curtly. "Five o'clock. Next week today."

"Okay," he said obediently. "I'll pick you up at Beach House?"

"It's called Beach Cove Inn." Only the girls were allowed to call it Beach House. That part of the house was private. Their own. Their home. Maisie's, and Ellie's, and Cate's and even Sam's, who Maisie said was just on borrowed time.

"Very original." The beginnings of a smirk started to lift his cheeks when he noticed her glance. "But also appropriate," Dale added hastily. "Very much in the local tradition. So I'll pick you up?"

"I'll drive myself. Where to?"

"What's good?"

"Your son's restaurant." Ellie watched him closely. He looked away, the upper-right corner of the store somehow catching his attention. "But let's not go there. He's got a job to do."

"Whatever you like. My treat."

Ellie almost snort-laughed at that. His treat? After he'd left her to starve in the store attic? It'd been her friends who'd made sure she was safe, not her husband. She inhaled and relaxed her clenched jaw.

"Harbor Shack."

"Yes. Yes, that's a good idea. Great. Erm—" Dale tilted his head and again tried his boyish smile.

Ellie knew he considered it the most swoonworthy weapon in his arsenal. To her, it just made Dale look like he wasn't able to find the breakfast cereal on his own. At their age, boyish didn't cut it anymore. "'Kay," she said, making sure ice frosted her words. "Bye. There's the door."

Dale's shoulders lifted as if he was going to argue, but then he dropped them again. "I can't wait," he said. "Bye, Ellilie. See you soon."

Ellie didn't wait. She stalked into the backroom, legs like stilts and neck hair bristling. When she was out of view, she set her hands flat on the metal counter, let her chin rest on her chest and took shallow breaths while she waited.

The store door swooshed air and shut with a soft pop.

Always, history had a way of catching up. Maisie had gone through it, finding Alex. Cate was going through it with Helene. And now her turn had come again.

Ellilie? He'd never called her that before. She didn't like it. She didn't feel very Ellilie toward him. Not one little bit.

Ellie straightened her back and pulled her phone from her jeans pocket. Her finger trembled as she swiped. "Tom?" She closed her eyes. "Your father's back in town."

Chapter 31

"How about the counter?" Em put a hand on the cool steel, trying not to sniff. There was still fish in the fridge, but the smell could be aired out. "Maybe we could keep it if we put the stoves in the corners instead."

It'd be great to fit both a convection and a double deck. A steamer would be fantastic, but how big were they again? She squinted at the corner, trying to picture the steamer. But she couldn't. She'd looked at too many appliances to remember. She patted the steel counter. It was nice and long and solid, just the thing she wanted. "I mean, we do need a counter. Makes no sense to rip it out if we can use it."

When she didn't get a response, she looked over her shoulder. "Tom?"

Tom let the measuring tape snap back and stood. "What?"

"We need a counter. It makes no sense to take this one out."

"We should think about a cake line, Em."

"A what?" Em asked. Commercial baking equipment was still unfamiliar to her. "What's a cake line for?"

"For making a high volume of donuts. The machine automates the process so you can do other things."

Em eyed him. He wasn't concentrating. All morning, he'd been distracted. "We said we'd stay away from donuts. People can buy them anywhere, even in the supermarket. We'll need a different signature. Like Maisie's cinnamon Franzbroetchen. Or a special cake. Mariner cake maybe, or molasses cake. Something with wild blueberries in the summer if we can find someone willing to pick."

Tom frowned. "We said that? Why don't I remember?"

Em crossed her arms. "The night at the Café? We talked about it over dinner."

"Ah, yes, the night at the Café." He nodded as if that explained it.

They'd had a brainstorming session that night. Alone in the empty restaurant, it'd been nearing midnight by the time all the chores were done and the place readied for the next day's business.

Tom baked one last pizza to share, while Em whipped up a bowl of chocolate mousse. Then Tom flipped off the lights so hungry late-night fishers wouldn't barge in and lit a candle on one of the tables. It was Em's favorite table, though she'd never told him. Sitting together in the dark, watching the crescent moon shine on the cove, their meeting felt safe and sweet and mysterious.

Eating hot pizza and cool mousse, they talked

about the new bakery until the early morning. Dawn rosied the fountain pool by the time they left, and the cool breeze smelled like home. Salty and bright and hopeful all at once.

Standing in the Fish Market, Em remembered thinking she could never be happy anywhere else but in Beach Cove.

How Tom had forgotten any of it was beyond Em. She herself recalled every word of their conversation, often going over it at night when she listened to Claire snoring on the futon.

"Are you okay, Tom?" she said. "You seem preoccupied. We can do this another time."

Tom slumped against the counter. "My dad's back in town." He rubbed his forehead. "Guess I am preoccupied. Sorry, Em."

He was her boss, but he was also her best friend. Em went to Tom and hugged him, burying her head in the nook between his neck and shoulder. "I told you he couldn't stay away from you," she whispered. "Nobody in their right mind can."

He reached up and put his hands on her shoulder, pushing her just far enough to look into her face. "No?"

"No." She smiled. "Whoever's going to fall for you is a lucky—is lucky." She'd almost said, 'lucky guy.' But he'd not come out yet, not even to her. Maybe he would do it now?

She waited for him to say more.

His smile faded. "Are you lucky, Em?" His hands slid down her arms to her fingers, and he gripped them.

Slowly, her heart aching for how hard it was for him to say it, Em leaned forward and kissed his cheek.

Sometime, she'd simply ask him whether he was gay. Sometime soon, she'd lance the boil and ask if he still loved Alex. But not now. Not here, where it smelled of fish and the light was clinical with steel and glass and sun pouring in the windows. Maybe they could have another sweet, slow night at the Café and talk.

Em stepped back and pulled her hands out of his. "Of course I am. Not as lucky as that, of course. But hey! I'm getting a bakery with you as my boss. If that's not lucky too, I don't know."

The words seemed to hang in the air between them like blocks of wood. Tom's face was a mask of stone. Clearly, Em had gotten too close to his secret. He wasn't ready yet. The barriers were still up.

Didn't he know she was always on his side? Always.

Em didn't understand what held him back. "You can talk to me, Tom," she finally said as gently as she could. "Just remember that we've been friends forever. For-*ever*. You know nothing's going to change that. Nothing at all."

"Ah." Tom pressed his lips together and nodded. "Thanks, Em. I appreciate you telling me."

"I'm sorry if you weren't sure. I should've said it earlier." Maybe his dad leaving had shaken Tom's trust in his relationships more than Em had realized. Maybe she should've told him earlier that he could always count on her. She smiled, relieved and glad she'd let him know what he needed to hear. Maybe now was after all his moment to open up. "Is there anything else you want to tell me?" she asked softly.

Tom studied his feet for too long. Then he pushed away from the counter and pulled out the tape measure. "Like I was saying. Dad's back."

Em was confused. How had he slipped through the net again? Didn't he *want* to unload? Didn't he want to share, get the secret off his chest? She followed him to the far corner.

"What are you measuring?"

"Uh—cake line?"

"Tom!" She lifted her open palms, exasperated. "We're not getting a cake line thing! Stop it."

Now he grinned. "It's for the stove, dummy. Take this and pull it all the way to the wall."

Em gripped the tape he handed her and did as she was told. "Are you going to meet Dale?"

"I guess." Tom scribbled numbers onto a notepad. "He's my dad. I'll have to sort things out with him sooner or later, so I might as well do it now."

"What are you going to say?" Em carried back her end of the tape so it wouldn't snap. Her finger touched Tom's when she let go. He flinched.

Em pulled a face. "Sorry! Did my fingernail scratch you?"

"No. Yes. It's fine." Tom shook out his hand as if he'd gotten a static shock. "I don't know. I guess I'll let Dad know what I think about men abandoning their families. Ask him why he did it." A crease appeared between his eyes.

Suddenly, Em couldn't speak. She nodded.

Mom had moved her and Claire's things into Beach House. Not the inn part, but the Jack and Jill in the main house where Ellie and Maisie lived.

"I'm sorry, Em," Tom said. "I'm sorry about the fire. Have they found out more?"

Em wrapped her arms around herself. "Mom's keeping things from me. Our house burned down, and she hasn't mentioned the fact that Dad's nowhere to be seen. As if I wouldn't notice."

Why wasn't Dad back to help Mom? Why hadn't he called them? Why wasn't there a family group text buzzing in the background? What was being swept under the rug?

"I don't know where he is," she murmured. Suddenly, the fish smell was overwhelming. She wasn't sure she could work here after all. Em covered her mouth until she was sure she wasn't going to be sick. "Sorry, Tom. I didn't mean to make it about me."

Tom frowned and opened the windows over the counter. "You have plenty of reason to make it about you. What do you think is going on?"

"That's just it. I really don't know." The fear that lived in Em's stomach since the night of the fire writhed like a snake. She pressed a hand against her midriff.

"Are you okay?"

"Ugh." Em swallowed. "I'm afraid…"

"What? Tell me, Em. You can trust me too, you know."

She exhaled a tight breath. True, he was the only person she could talk to. She could tell him things she couldn't even tell Mom. Especially Mom.

"I'm afraid Dad's got something to do with the fire," she whispered. It felt horrible saying it out loud. But at night when she lay sleepless, staring at the ceiling of her new bedroom, the thought circled her like a shark. "Usually he texts Claire and me every couple of days to see what we're up to. Now, nothing. I mean, anything could've happened in that fire. It's a big deal."

"Cate hasn't talked with him since?"

"She says she has."

"You don't believe her?"

It wasn't that easy. "She's behaving strangely. Different. Maybe it's the shock? I don't know. I think she's trying to avoid me."

Tom smiled. "No way. She'd not avoid you for anything in the world."

But Mom wasn't in touch, not the way she usually was. It took her forever to answer texts. She'd practically sent Claire to stay with Em, even though Claire loved Beach House and wanted to sleep there.

"I can't tell what's going on. And that's an understatement."

"I can try and find out more," Tom offered after a pause. "My mom probably knows what's going on with your mom. I'm sure they're all talking to each other."

They probably did. They always did. It wasn't the first time they'd fed the kids only select bits of what was happening.

Em smiled. "Okay. Sure. Thanks."

Tom winked at her. "Anytime."

"So…" Em sighed. "Sorry. What about Dale?"

"Oh. Oh." Tom waved the air away. "Forget Dale. I'll ask him a few questions, is all."

For a moment, they looked at each other, smiling, glad the other was there. At least Em was. Her stomach was better. She wanted a hug, but she didn't want to be a baby.

"Dad and Allen are responsible for their choices," Tom said earnestly. "They'll have to deal with the consequences."

"True."

"We all do," he repeated quietly. "We make choices and have to deal with the consequences."

Em thought they would talk more about Dale, and where her dad might be, but Tom, tape in hand, started crawling around on the floor, ducking under and behind things as he measured and scribbled notes.

Clearly, he'd had enough heart-to-heart for a day.

Feeling useless, Em sat on the counter and let her legs dangle. What would Alex have said about the fire and her dad's absence? Em wanted to know. She inhaled to ask Tom, but when she looked up, he'd disappeared entirely. Metal clanged in the front of the store.

Em blew the air out. It was better not to bring up Alex anyway.

She didn't want Tom pulling out his cigarettes

again.

Em started to take photos of the back room, the walls and windows, trying to imagine the cute small-town bakery where neighbors bought their bagels and met for a coffee, a cookie and a chat.

Despite the lingering smell, Ellie was wrapping up her business, selling the last of her wares and planning a little goodbye beach party. It was the end of an era, Em thought. Ellie had shaped everything around them.

Em loved Tom's mom—and now Em's job was to dismantle what Ellie had built. A pang of longing for the old days hit her like a sneaky wave.

Alex had been alive, and they'd been little. Ellie, Maisie, Cate and Sam had casually handed out snacks and wiped noses and shouted for them to get in or out of the water, all the while talking to each other.

It'd been easy back then.

It was complicated now.

Em let her phone sink. "You okay over there, Tom?" she called out quietly. "We can come back tomorrow. Do you want to get out?"

"Sort of."

"I can't concentrate at all."

"Me neither."

"Let's go have lunch," Em suggested. They could let things be for an hour. Talk about other things than fire or abandonment. "They have mussels and french fries at the Shack today. We can feed the gulls."

Tom appeared at the door. "I like gulls."

Em smiled. "I like gulls too."

Chapter 32

Maisie paused at the top of the beach stairs and shaded her eyes. A soft evening sun hung over the coast, and not a breath of wind moved the sea. Like sea glass, it shimmered in opaque shades of blue and green and turquoise, reflecting color onto sand and sky.

A few hundred steps away, Vince and Will stood at the waterline. In tribute to the heat, they wore a uniform of linen pants and white button-downs, sleeves rolled to the elbow. Watches glinted identical on their wrists, though Will wore a baseball cap while Vince's mane was uncovered, and Will's bare feet stood in the glassy water while Vince stood on the wet sand where beach and sea unite.

It was the day of Will's departure, and the two men looked deep in conversation. Time for tea and cake had come and passed, and neither one of them had come to the patio. Maisie and Ellie had sat by themselves, and once they'd finished their slice of molasses cake—Em's courtesy—Ellie had excused herself.

She had the store-closing party coming up and had whisked Cate off to Seaside Bay, where they had a beauty salon. Maisie had stayed at the inn in case Will needed anything. Since he'd paid before ever stepping foot in the house, she figured she should at least make sure his car arrived for the ride to the airport.

Maisie let her hand sink. Had the two men been here since this morning, deep in conversation as they walked the beach for hours?

What were they talking about?

There'd been times throughout his visit when Will had disappeared. Neither Maisie nor Ellie had been able to find out where he went. When asked, Will talked about surrounding villages in convincing detail.

But Will had been dropped off at the inn on the day of his arrival. He didn't have a car for trips. And when she'd brought Vince a bouquet of lavender for the kitchen table, Maisie had noticed that *his* car hadn't moved for trips to neighboring villages either.

Not that it was any of her business.

Just mild curiosity. It was a small town, after all.

And so, casually, just to stave off boredom, Maisie and Ellie had made inquiries. None of the Beach Cove store owners could report having seen Will. Neither the barista who made crepes nor Tom had seen the men in the village.

Had Will lied? He could do as he pleased. There was no reason to make up stories.

Maisie sat on the top stair and hugged her knees, admiring the sea, the preening cotton puff clouds, the delicate pattern of shells on sand.

If it were possible, would she eavesdrop on the

men's conversation?

She didn't know. Maybe. But there wasn't a place less conducive to eavesdropping than the beach. There was no cover to hide. Even if one would sneak up on the men somehow, which one naturally didn't and wouldn't ever, it'd be impossible to listen in.

Just because the cove was a quiet mirror didn't mean the rushing Atlantic behind the cliffs was too. Like a running faucet or a radio tuned to static, it was stellar at preventing words from being overheard.

"Maisie? What are you doing?"

Maisie startled. She'd started to dream, her eyes becoming unfocused as they scanned the horizon. "Vince. Hey, Will." She squinted up at them, wiping the white sand from her legs. "I came for a walk, but I didn't want to interrupt you."

Will nodded, but Vince's smile traveled to his eyes.

"Thank you, my dear. Will and I are out of time, and it was necessary to catch up." He offered his hand. It was large and tan, the nails immaculate, the palm hard from working the apple orchard.

Maisie took it.

Vince helped her rise but didn't let go, pulling her much closer than she'd expected. Maisie could smell the scent of fragrant tea always lingering on him, the leather of his wristwatch, the linen shirt, the beach in his hair, the tan of his warm skin, and when she looked up she knew he'd waited for her to meet his gaze.

Maisie's heart hitched, missing a beat. Because she'd waited for him to meet her gaze, too.

Finally, Will moved and said something.

Then Maisie was suddenly able to move again herself, and she looked down and stepped back, knowing the warmth in her cheeks and her chest had nothing to do with the evening sun.

"I better go check I haven't forgotten anything in my room," Will said. He was smiling at her. "I'll see you soon."

"Of course," Maisie managed to say. Wasn't she going back, too? Or was she going to stay here on the beach with Vince?

She turned to look at her friend and neighbor, but his eyes were on Will's face, communicating something over her head.

"Maybe I'll take my walk after all," she said, noticing a small breeze coming in from the water. It ruffled the smooth surface into patterns.

Will bowed, and then he turned and strode up the path that led through the jumbled wildflowers to the house.

"Shall we?" Vince said casually, as if it were perfectly understood they should walk together. He offered his arm.

Again, Maisie's heart skipped a few beats. She tried to take a deep breath, but even without extra air her insides suddenly fluttered like the fledgling wrens in her rhododendron.

Was this how it was? Was this how it was even after fifty?

Maisie took Vince's arm, her fingertips coming to rest on the bare skin between watch and sleeve.

"All right?" Vince asked.

"All right," Maisie answered, and he led her onto the beach and into the sand and down to the sea where their feet marked a narrow path.

They didn't speak. Maisie didn't think she could.

Before the kiss, they'd often walked arm in arm. Maisie had enjoyed being with Vince, but she'd still been Robert's wife and widow.

Until she'd felt Vince's lips on her own.

Of course she knew the kiss in the apple orchard hadn't been an accident. Vince had asked what she wanted, and Maisie had found she wanted him.

The way he'd looked at her moments ago, the way he'd pulled her close when she rose from the stairs, even the way Will had smiled and left, told Maisie that Vince wanted her too. More than before. She didn't think that this time, he meant to ask.

And unlike before, touching his arm now jolted her with a charge that widened her eyes and locked her lungs and zapped her skin with a shock as powerful as Puck's magic-sweet flower.

Lightly, Maisie moved her fingers over his arm, letting them stretch and curl like kittens so she could feel more of his skin, the hard muscle underneath, more hair, more heat.

Vince inhaled a breath that was louder than the rippling waves and glanced at her hand. But he didn't stop walking, or stop her, or help her.

"Don't worry about seeing off Will," he said after a while. "Someone is coming to pick him up."

Maisie nodded. She could barely concentrate. And

yet, who was that someone coming to pick up Will? Slowly, gradually, she stopped the movement of her fingers. It was possible she had it wrong after all; maybe she was projecting her feelings.

Maybe Vince was simply walking her away from seeing someone. And maybe he had a good reason for doing so.

"I don't worry, Vince," she replied when her words returned to her. "I understand."

A small wave swelled higher than the last, crested and broke and softly washed over their naked toes, inviting them to come with it, back into the sea.

Vince let Maisie go, and she looked at him. He held her gaze, and then he took her hands, circling her wrists with his fingers as if they were handcuffs and she was his prisoner, bringing them to his heart. His smile vanished and a crease folded between his eyes, a frown of something Maisie couldn't process.

Vince rested her hands on his chest and slid his own up her arms, pushing the loose sleeves of her blouse higher, tracing the sensitive crook of the elbow where the blood runs just below the skin.

Maisie thought he'd pull her to him and that it would be a release from his eyes, but Vince wasn't done. With two fingers he traced her throat, the line of her jaw, the hollow of her cheek, and then he suddenly spread his hands and cradled her head between them.

With the slightest pressure, he could tilt her mouth. With the slightest bend of his head, he could bring his lips to hers.

Maisie drew a ragged breath, but her lungs

rejected it, sending it back to part her lips and escape.

Vince's nostrils flared as if he were a hunter catching her scent, and he leaned down and pressed his lips to Maisie's forehead.

Maisie closed her eyes to his scent, his mouth, his power and presence. She couldn't move, but she wanted more; she wanted to feel his lips on her own, feel their insistence, know that it was perfect.

But Vince didn't kiss her again. Instead he pulled her to him, close so she could hear his beating heart. "My love," he murmured. Only that. Only once.

"Yes," Maisie whispered to his heart. "I'm here."

For a time, they stood silent. Then, Vince stirred and released her. "We'd better go back to the house."

Maisie looked up and caught an expression of regret on his face. She stood, studying his features. He looked different. His eyes were wide open and blue, his lips animated, the lines of his face clean and straight. The mask was off. He was allowing her to see him, but she knew it was only for a little while.

What would happen if she kissed him now? She still felt the pressure of his thumb in her elbow, his finger tracing her lip.

He could hide, but for how much longer?

Maisie didn't know.

"Okay," she said. "You're right. Let's go back and see whether Will's been picked up."

Chapter 33

Built from red brick and white wood, the police station looked as modern as the nearby fire station. The buildings were far from the historic village with its cute markets and shops, and Cate rarely passed by here. Squinting at the staple, she realized the police station was even newer than Beach Cove High.

Cate lifted her heavy tote higher. Then she pushed open the glass door and walked into the building.

The air was moist and smelled of wax and polish. The linoleum floor had recently been mopped; a yellow cone still warned of slipping. Compared to the bright sunny day outside, the light seemed dim.

A woman appeared at the window to Cate's left, peering through the glass. "Can I help you, ma'am?"

Cate smiled tensely, and when she spoke, her voice was thin with nerves. There'd be consequences for what she was about to do. She didn't know what would happen, but it was possible she'd be in serious trouble. "I'd like to see someone about the fire a few nights ago," she said. "It was my house that burned."

"I know," the woman said, "I saw the damage. Crazy."

Cate thought she'd seen the woman before. Maybe in the grocery store or at the beach.

"I'm Inga Parson. Lilly's mom," the woman said. "Lilly loved having you in English. She's never been one for the books, and I was sure that train had sailed. But you got her reading; did you know that? You changed her mind."

"Oh, of course!" Prompted, Cate saw the similarities in the high cheekbones and the shape of the generous mouth. Sweet, rebellious Lilly had been one of Cate's favorites; she'd been determined to hate English but hadn't held out long against the stories they'd selected together. "It was a joy to have Lilly in class," Cate said. "Let her know, would you? And if she'd like to read the last book in the series, I can give it to her. It finally came out."

"She was so sad when she heard you quit," Inga said. "It's a loss for the school."

"I didn't quit. I took a sabbatical," Cate said. One she wished she'd never agreed to. "But I already miss my students. I'll be back next semester if I can."

"Too late for Lilly," Inga Parson said with a mixture of regret and accusation. "Well, let me get you someone to talk to about the fire. Just a moment."

"Thanks, Mrs. Parson." Cate sat on the orange plastic chair below the window and pulled the tote on her lap.

The opposite wall was painted the same yellow as the classrooms of Beach High. There was also a stand with a thriving spider plant to look at.

Helene would be back in Hollywood now. Running

her agency, meeting with actors and singers over fancy lunches and expensive dinners and too much gin. She'd not gotten in touch yet. She probably needed time to process all that had happened. But then she would call.

"Cate?"

Cate startled. "Sophia." She stood.

Sophia had led the recovery of Alex's remains. Earlier, she'd spearheaded the last few years of investigation into his disappearance, following up on tips and alleged sightings. Still in her forties, Cate thought of Sophia as an already seasoned investigator.

Years ago, Sophia had interviewed Cate about Alex and his friendship with Em. Back then, the smile had been wider. Warmer. More genuine.

Cate dropped her gaze. "I'd like to talk with someone about the fire. And something else." This wasn't for Inga Parson's ears.

"Sure. Come this way, Cate."

Sophia led her down the corridor into a small office. There were no pictures or plants, only a computer on a desk and a gray metal filing cabinet. She pointed to a chair like in the hall; this one was blue. Maybe the chairs were color-coded.

"Thanks." Cate sat. The stiff denim waistband of her jeans dug into her belly, but at least the button stayed closed. For a moment, she wished she'd worn something comfortable.

Sophia rounded the desk and sat in her own chair. "What can I do for you, Cate?"

"You know about the fire?" Cate moistened her lip.

Sophia nodded. "I do." She drummed a finger on the desk. "Tell me what's on your mind. I'll make sure it reaches the right people."

"Okay." Cate had expected to meet the two officers who'd stopped by her house. Sophia couldn't do it all on her own. But maybe she did. She too looked tired, with shadows under her eyes.

"Every detail is important." Sophia leaned forward. "Did you remember anything, Cate? Do you know who started the fire in your house?"

Cate shook her head. "Not exactly. But I know it wasn't Allen if that's who you suspect."

Sophia leaned back, her face blank. "How do you know it wasn't him? Have you seen him?"

"No. No, I have no idea where he is." Cate hastened on before Sophia could interrupt. "He called me."

"He called you? When?"

"The night of the fire, actually."

Sophia dug her bottom teeth into her upper lip, looking deep in thought. "You didn't tell us, Cate."

"You didn't ask," Cate answered. "Nobody's asked me anything."

"Oh. I thought they talked to you. They should've."

"Two police officers came to my house, but that was before the fire happened. Of course they wanted to talk about something else. About Allen. Where he'd been."

Sophia's eyes didn't leave Cate's face. "I heard he was at home with you."

"Back then—" Cate gasped to draw a breath. "I might not have told them everything back then,

Sophia. I hope—" Hand shaking, Cate lifted the tote bag on the desk.

She hoped the lie she'd told on Allen's behalf hadn't done real damage. She didn't know how significant it was. What he'd really done.

But after the way he'd exposed her and Claire to danger, Cate thought Allen could've done anything. Anything at all.

By giving him an alibi, she'd made herself an accomplice. That's what they called people like her. An accomplice.

She'd walked into the station knowing she might not walk out.

Cate clutched the chair under the desk to have something to hold on to. "I'm… I don't know where he was, Sophia." She swallowed. No more lies. No more excuses. "He'd been gone. He hadn't been home, the way I told your colleagues."

"You gave him an alibi," Sophia said. "A false alibi. For a time when he was seen somewhere else. We needed to know if it was him that day, but because of you, we couldn't be sure. Our investigation stalled."

Cate nodded. Shame welled up again, throttling her throat, but she breathed it away. "I never should've covered for him. I know. I knew back then too. Only…"

"Only he made you?" Sophia said it kindly. There was no trace of sarcasm in her voice.

"He said he'd fallen asleep at the wheel and smashed into a shop window." Cate's voice was firm. She'd wanted to say this. She'd wanted to say this ever since the two cops pulled into her driveway.

"When did he say it happened?" Sophia opened a drawer and pulled out a notepad. "Okay if I write this down?"

Cate nodded, and then she gave Sophia the dates when Allen had been gone and repeated the window story he'd told her.

When Sophia was done jotting notes, she put the pen down. "He's said something else, hasn't he?"

Cate gripped the seat of her chair.

"Tell me what it was, Cate."

It was the look on Sophia's face that made Cate speak. "It's silly, Sophia. Nothing."

"Why don't you let me decide?"

Cate pulled air into her lungs. Where did excuse stop and abuse start? "It's just—he said I should lie for our marriage. And the girls."

Sophia chewed the inside of her lip. "Emily and Claire, right?"

"Yes. Yes. I thought... If he and I were on the same page, I thought we could be happy. Be happier." Cate's fingers hurt, and she released her grip on the edge of the chair. "I knew it wasn't... I knew it wasn't real, Sophia. I knew it wouldn't work. But I kept telling myself I was wrong, that I just wasn't working hard enough for his love and respect. That I could still catch up with my dreams and have a good marriage and happy children."

Sophia let her head drop into her neck. Then she straightened again. "Cate, you were scared. Scared of your husband. Is that right?"

Cate's blood pulsed loud in her ears as the feeling

came back to her. "That's right," she admitted quietly.

Sophia stood and went to the window, then came to sit on the corner of the desk. "Where is Allen, Cate?"

Cate shook her head. "I asked, but he won't say." She told Sophia about the call after the fire. "He hasn't answered his phone since," she finished. "It goes straight to voice mail."

Sophia sat a while longer, thinking. Then she said, "Excuse me," and left the room, closing the door behind her.

Cate held her breath. It was better than hyperventilating.

It took Sophia an eternity to come back, though Cate knew only five minutes had ticked by on the clock.

"Sorry about that," Sophia said. "All right. Let me tell you something for a change."

Cate put a hand to her heart. It was beating so hard, she thought everyone could see it.

"There's a warrant out for your husband. We've been trying to find him for a while."

"There was no shop window, was there?" Cate felt dizzy. Disembodied. The way it felt when one reality clashed with another.

Sophia pulled a bottle of water from a drawer in her desk. "It's warm, but you should drink some. You look like you're about to faint."

Cate took the water, staring at the little white cap. "I'm so ashamed for having lied to the police. For trying so hard to believe Allen. You have no idea how ashamed I am."

"Maybe I do. I've known you for years, after all. And I know abuse when I see it."

"He never hit me. He never cursed or called me names." Besides fat. And stupid, sometimes. And sometimes, he'd grabbed her hard. But the marks had long gone, and she couldn't prove anything. Not the way she could prove the cigarette burn.

"He didn't have to," Sophia said gently.

After a while, Cate asked, "What did he do?"

Sophia went back to her chair. "If I tell you, will you help us?"

"I will help you either way, Sophia. That's why I came."

Sophia nodded. "He's been running a Ponzi scheme."

"A what?" Cate had heard the name before, but her brain drew a blank.

"He gets people to invest in his business. We're talking a lot of money here, Cate. Allen keeps a nice chunk for himself. He uses the rest to pay off investors and bring new ones on board."

"Oh." Cate had never seen any money. "I don't know what to say," she said helplessly. "I've always paid for the household and kids with my own salary."

"I believe you, though we'll have to check. It'd be easier if you cooperated."

"Of course. Whatever you need."

"Ponzi schemes are illegal," Sophia said earnestly. "Nothing of value is produced. Sooner or later, investors get cheated out of their money." She leaned forward. "Besides committing a crime, Allen cheated the wrong people."

Cate sat still, stunned. "That's the reason for the fire?"

Sophia shrugged.

"It makes sense." It felt as if she'd been jolted awake; Cate sat up straight as pieces shifted and fit together. "It does make sense. There were men watching the house. I thought…"

Sophia picked up her pen. "Did you see their faces?"

"Yes." Cate tried to remember. "Yes, I did see their faces. There was also a kid that picked up Allen on that last trip…" She described the faces of the men and the young driver with the hoodie and the hard eyes.

"Good, Cate," Sophia said when she was done writing. "Anything else you can give us?"

Cate pointed to the bag. "I have the hard drive from Allen's computer."

Sophia shook her head as if she hadn't heard correctly. "*You* took the computer?"

"Um…yes. I went back into the house the morning after the fire. I didn't want Allen to get it first." Cate blinked guiltily.

Sophia pressed her lips together. "They should've collected it before you were allowed back in."

"Well, it's in the tote if you still want it. I haven't done anything other than go into Allen's files and make copies for safekeeping. You'll see the dates." Cate thought for a moment. "He's kept track of everything. I didn't know what the numbers meant." She shook her head. "But it would make sense with…what you said. If they were transactions. Maybe you can check against the money people invested."

Sophia pulled the bag close and peeked inside. "What's in the file folders?"

"Anything I could find on his trips. There are receipts from gas stations and restaurants and such and a couple of folders with forms he kept."

Sophia's eyes widened as she rifled through the pages. "Bank documents."

Cate nodded. "I couldn't make sense of it. I never thought it was his money because the accounts are in different names."

Sophia took the bag. "Sit tight." She disappeared again. When she came back, she said, "They're going to keep it all. Is that okay?"

"Yes," Cate said. For the first time since she'd entered the station, she could take a deep breath. "That's okay."

"Anything else?"

Cate hesitated. "How much trouble am I in?"

"No idea, Cate. I'll put in a word and see what I can do. It was good you came but get a lawyer just in case." Sophia smiled.

"Only..." Cate rubbed her cheek with a hand. "Claire's still with me. She just turned seventeen."

"Oh. Well." Sophia stood. "I'm sure she won't grow up motherless. I can't tell you anything concrete, but my guess is you'll get a chance to tell your side."

Cate stood too. She could tell her story. She'd known nothing about the Ponzi scheme; she had none of Allen's money. Her stomach lifted with relief. "I'll call him again," she promised. "I'll get him to tell me where he is. And when I do, I'll let you know."

Sophia opened the door for Cate and walked her down the corridor. At the front door, she stopped, hand on the handle. "I can't stop you from calling your husband," she said. "But if you want my advice, don't do it. Let us deal with him; the material you gave me should help track him down. He's involved with people I'd like to keep as far as possible from you and your girls."

"Allen doesn't care about us. Hurting us isn't going to hurt him. I hope they realize that."

Sophia followed her outside. "Still, keep an eye out. Just in case. Any more men in cars watching you, you let me know."

"Thank you, Sophia." Cate blinked into the sun. Was this how it felt to be reborn? Light and bright and unafraid even though mobsters might be out to get her? "Let me know if I can help."

Sophia checked over her shoulder, and then she quickly reached out and hugged Cate. "You did good today, Cate. I'm glad. This is going to make my life a lot easier."

"Mine too," Cate said, the words coming from the bottom of her heart.

It was time to go home. Ellie and Maisie were waiting for her. Together they would have tea on the patio, in the sun, sampling Em's baking, and discussing what just happened.

For the first time in a long time, Cate really relaxed. It wasn't over; she realized that. The arsonists were still out there. And there'd be a trial once they caught Allen.

But Ellie knew how to get a divorce. Maisie had an excellent lawyer. And Sam had a feel for the right thing to do.

Never again would Cate fall for a narcissist.

Instead, for the first time ever, she was going to live life on her own terms. As a mother of daughters, a sister, a friend and a teacher.

As a woman in her own right.

Chapter 34

"Here. You'll need this. I know I do."

Sam took the glass of chardonnay Ellie offered. "Thanks. Happy fish retirement, my dear." They clinked glasses, and Sam sipped the cool golden liquid. Her truck was parked in the driveway of Beach House, and Sam meant to drive it back home later. The glass should last the evening.

Ellie was still drinking, her eyes closed and her throat moving with intent. Sam loosened the top button of her shirt and scanned the beach left and right. She'd never seen it this crowded. There were lots of people from the village and even one or two faces Sam didn't recognize. Everyone was dressed in bright colors and linen and shimmering party dresses. Not a single person wore shoes.

When at last Ellie let her glass sink to smack her lips in a content but unladylike manner, Sam had to grin. "Hey, Ells. Cheers."

"Cheers. It's the end of an era, Sammy. Tonight, I do what I want."

Sam felt her grin widen. Ellie was already tipsy. "Go right on ahead," Sam said supportively, then pointed at the crowd. "Looks like a lot of people are glad to see you retire." Or everyone remembered Maisie's legendary beach parties.

"Haha. Funny." Ellie shook her head, sending her curls flying and her dress twinkling. It was a silver number Sam hadn't seen before. In the glow of the fairy lights strung around the canopies, the large sequins shimmered like scales. Ellie stabbed a finger in the air. "But you're wrong. Everyone came because they love me."

Sam nodded, biting back the comment that it was a pity they didn't eat seafood on top of loving Ells. "I love you too, Ellie," she said instead. Ellie wasn't likely to remember, so it was okay to go a little mushy. "I think it's great you're taking things into your hands and changing track to do what you enjoy. It's not easy, and it takes courage and strength of character. Well done, sweets."

"I don't know, sweets." Ellie hiccupped. "That's what you call a kid with Gerber cheeks. Also, don't think I won't remember you getting all mushy on me." She made a fist and play-boxed Sam's arm, surprisingly steady. "I'll hold you to it tomorrow, witch."

Sam rubbed the spot. "You try and do that, fish."

Ellie looked down her dress and wiggled her hips to set the sequins swinging. "Mermaid, dude. I'm going for mermaid."

Sam drew herself up. "I *doubt* you're going to remember—"

"But I love you too," Ellie interrupted her.

Sam narrowed her eyes, ready for battle. Or bottle, rather. "Can I refresh you?" she offered casually. "I'll just go get—"

"Nice try. No." Ellie shook her head and drained her glass. "I do what I want, and now I want water—oh. Uh-oh."

"What?" Sam swiveled on her heel in the warm sand.

"Nothing."

"Gordy? You invited Gordy?"

"No. Well, I didn't *not* invite him. I put up a flyer in the store window. Anyone walking by could read it." Ellie put her glass on a table, and a waiter immediately refilled it. "Oh no, I don't... Fine. Good." She picked it up again and sighed. "Maisie told them to do that."

Sam turned back. "Do you want me to go and tell him to leave? He'll never again sell me one of his really superb lobster rolls, but I'll do it for you. It's your party. You get to enjoy yourself."

"Uh." Ellie glanced in Gordy's direction. "No. It's all right. Actually..." She sidled up to Sam as if getting ready to confess a sin. "He came to the store."

"He came to the store? Gordy? *Your* store?"

Ellie blinked yes.

"Interesting," Sam murmured. Gordy was definitely looking over at them. And he had something in his hand. If Sam hadn't gone blind, it was a single red carnation. "Interesting," she murmured again.

Ells and Gordy had been sworn enemies since they first laid eyes on each other.

Sam lowered her head closer to Ellie. "Well, don't leave me hanging," she said. "What did he want?"

"I'm not so sure." Ellie shifted her weight. "I mean, he said—"

"Uh-OH." Sam let her glass sink. "I don't mean to interrupt the scoop on your and Gordy's latest mano-a-mano, but I'll be darned if that's not your ex over there."

Ellie gushed out a breath as if she'd been punched. "What?"

"That's *Dale*. Oh no, Ellie, he's coming over. Quick. What do you want to do?"

"I told him not to mess with me." Ellie took another swig.

Dale was close enough to see them now, and Sam quickly turned her head. "Hey, not to make this worse or anything," she whispered, "but Gordy's coming over here, too. And he's got a flower for you." Then Ellie's words trickled through, and Sam opened her eyes, incredulous. "What do you mean you told Dale not to mess with you? You've been talking to him? Since when?"

"He came to the store, too." Ellie opened her eyes again. "Okay, Sam, go get Maisie. You'll just get mad at Dale. I need a cool head to help me with this one."

The two men were still advancing, their eyes on Sam's shimmering friend. "Will do," Sam promised. "Hang in there."

"Ellilie? You look fantastic!"

Dale's voice made Sam's spine crawl sideways. What was going on between him and Ellie?

"I came to wish you all the best. I was hoping we could talk," Gordy's baritone rung out.

Ellie looked at Sam with scared eyes. "Run," she whispered.

"Like the wind." Maybe Maisie knew more. Sam backed into the crowd of Beach Covians. She nodded at a gloomy Madame Botrel who clearly contemplated a future without the Fish Market, waved at Tom and Em, who wore aprons and lugged trays of caviar toast and bruschetta, and swerved around kids whose church best was already ruined by saltwater.

"Who are you looking for?" Cate appeared from the crowd.

Sam stopped dead. Cate was dressed in a gauzy sea-glass green dress that flowed freely from bust to feet. Her milky shoulders and décolletage were—
"*Goodness.*" Sam blinked several times. "You look like the lead in one of those chest-hoisting Regency dramas."

"I kind of love it," Cate admitted, sheepishly glancing down herself. "I've had it forever but never wore it."

"Well, you look..." Sam shook her head, unable to process the sight.

Crystals glittered in Cate's ears and a necklace of tiny crystal flowers and pearls twinkled on her neck. Together with the short, silvery hair, Cate looked like a queen.

"Honestly, I didn't know you could look like that," Sam admitted.

Cate fingered the necklace. "Too much? Too

weird? Maisie made me put on her diamonds. I knew they were over the top. I've got clothes to change; I can go and..." She pointed over her shoulder at Beach House.

"No!" Sam held her hands up. "No, it looks *gorgeous*, Cate. You're an absolute triumph. Whatever you do, don't change out of this dress. Gotta give people a minute to wrap their mind around the transformation though."

Cate chuckled. "Since I'm starting over, I thought this time I should do what I want."

"I've heard that one before," Sam muttered. "Hey, have you seen Maisie by chance?"

"Ah." Cate played with a bracelet that seemed to spark fire. "Um. Yes. She's over there." She pointed to the edge of the illuminated area.

"What's she doing over there in the dark?" Sam tried to lift on tiptoes to see over the heads, but the sand under her feet gave way. "Cate, is that... Are they..."

Maisie sat on a bench beside Vince, their heads tilted toward each other, their eyes on the moon. Vince was holding Maisie's hand. Their fingers were intertwined, and her free hand rested on his arm.

Cate smiled. "Whatever it is, it looks like the sweetest thing in the world. Don't you think?"

Sam turned away. "But is it a good idea?"

"They seem happy."

"But we don't know anything about Vince," Sam said. "What's going on in the basement? What is he doing down there?"

"He's catching mice."

"Come on, Cate. He's *not* catching *mice*."

Again, Cate smiled. "Sam. He's catching mice. Okay? *Look* at her."

Vince was speaking, his lips moving, and Maisie laughed quietly.

"I'd *think*," Sam said, "you of all people would like to know exactly what sort of mice he's catching. What about your new policy of full disclosure?"

"I don't believe he's going to set her house on fire," Cate replied calmly, her eyes on the couple. "Do you?"

Sam held up her hands, exasperated. "Does it matter?"

Cate's smile turned wry. "If you'd been the one waking up to a fire threatening your sister, you'd think so."

Sam sighed. "Sorry. I don't want anything to happen to Maisie. She's been through enough."

Cate patted Sam's hand. "Maisie's a big girl. She can do what she wants."

"Seems to be the motto of the night."

One of the local teens hired to help bumped into Sam. "Hey," she said ungraciously. "Watch it."

"Sorry, Mrs. Bowers. Sorry." The boy edged nervously around her. "This is for you, Mrs. Clark. And my mom says to say hi."

"Thank you, Kevin. Say hi to her too. I loved the cookies."

"She'll make more," Kevin said resignedly. "See ya, Mrs. Clark."

"Bye." Cate turned the letter over. "His dad's the

mail carrier," she explained. "Sometimes I get my mail early."

"Okay." Sam wasn't surprised. After Dale, Gordy, Vince and Cate's dress, nothing was going to surprise her. "Who's it from?"

"My sister." Cate ripped open the envelope.

Sam recognized the same stationary Dale had used to write to Bonnie. "It's from the Sandpiper Inn. She wrote it before she left."

Cate took a while to read. The envelope fluttered to the floor, and Sam picked it up. When she looked back at Cate, she knew something was wrong.

"What's the matter? Is Helene okay?"

Mute, Cate held out the letter.

Cate, Sam read.

Thanks for being there when I needed you. You had no reason to help.

I have more questions. I don't know what they are, but they'll come to me. Right now, my past seems to be wrapped in quicksand and paper, and I'll have to dig and tear before I understand what happened.

But I remember you again, Cate, even though I forgot. I too know you in a way no one else can because I was there in those stolen childhood moments when no one was watching, and we could be ourselves. I hold on to those moments, because I know they were real.

I want to return what should be yours. I don't need it, and I think it'll be useful to you.

Your sister,

Helene

"That's nice," Sam mumbled.

"I'm glad she's back in my life."

Sam cleared her throat. She knew she tended to be overprotective of her friends. She hadn't liked Helene much nor given her a proper chance. But it was obvious Cate was better off with her sister. "She writes you two still have more talking to do."

"She wants to do the work," Cate said and took the letter back. "That's all I can do, too."

"What is she returning?" Sam felt the envelope and held it out. "There's more in there."

Cate took it. "I don't know." She shook the envelope open and pulled out a slip of paper. "Oh. It's a check."

"For what?"

Cate stared at the print. It took her a while to answer. "She says on the memo line it's my half of the inheritance."

Sam had a vague memory of knowing Cate's parents had been wealthy. How wealthy, she didn't know. But Cate could use a little money. Claire's college wasn't going to be easy on a teacher's salary, and Allen wasn't likely to pitch in. "Um," she said when she couldn't stand it any longer. "Is it a lot?"

Cate turned over the check so Sam could see.

Sam's eyes widened, then watered. It was a lot. A *lot* a lot.

"Sheesh." She blew out a breath. "For real?"

Cate shrugged, helpless. "Dad did well. He was always working."

Sam held out the check. "Goodness, Cate. Please tell me you're going to take it." It was more money than Cate's burned-down house was worth, more than Sam's store and Ellie's store and all their houses put together.

Cate took the paper and folded it. "I will," she said thoughtfully. "Mother didn't want me to have it, but Helene does. I think she means it. I'll make sure."

Sam nodded. "Good girl. You do deserve it, my dear. Congratulations."

Cate took a breath that threatened to split her dress. "Excuse me, Sam. I think I'm going to get Claire. I'm also going to call Helene. I want to thank her for the letter and ask if she's serious about the money."

Sam helped track down Claire, who was blond and bubbly and surrounded by a gaggle of teens, and then watched Cate and her walk arm in arm over the sand toward the house. Mother and daughter looked bright and beautiful in the moonlight. Maybe they even looked a little rich.

What else was going to happen tonight? Sam swirled her wine and set the glass on the nearest table even though it was still half full. She'd had enough.

Then she remembered her original mission and craned her neck to see whether Gordy and Dale were still with Ellie.

They were. The three of them formed a triangle, with Dale and Gordy staring at each other. Ellie was looking at her empty glass.

Sam glanced to the other side. Vince had put an arm around Maisie, and her head rested on his shoulder. Maisie couldn't see it, but Vince was studying her face, clearly very much in love.

Okay, it really was pretty sweet, and they'd all known it was coming. So now the only one—

"Samantha?"

"Yes?" Rubbing her neck, Sam turned.

A tall stranger with a cut jawline, sapphire eyes and silver temples smiled at her. "Hi."

"Hi." Sam swallowed.

"I've been searching for you forever. I'm Dave."

Sam stared at the hand he held out. It was large and tempting and could very well belong to an artist. Or a scammer. She shook it, just to see how it felt to the touch. "Which Dave? My *cousin*?"

Like all scammers, the man had the most charming smile. It was all dimple and tooth and heart. "Your very, very distant cousin. How are you?"

Sam pulled her hand out of his. She felt a lot warmer than the mild evening and her short dress warranted. "I don't know," she said weakly. "I just don't know right now."

The smile slipped. "Please, take my arm," Dave said. "Let me help you."

"Okay." That was fine; a girl on her own could deal with only so much in a night. Sam slipped her arm through that of her very, very distant cousin and found him to be solid, steady and smelling of printed paper and pottery clay.

"You're hot." He tightened the angle of his arm, pulling her closer. "How do you feel about a glass of chilled chardonnay, my dear?"

Sam smiled. She'd always liked her relatives. "I don't mind if I do," she said.

Note to the Reader

Dear Reader – I hope you enjoyed Beach Cove Sisters. You can find out how the story continues in book four of the series, Beach Cove Secrets.

Stay in touch at subscribepage.com/nelliebrooks and be the first to know about new releases, sales, and promos. You can find me on Facebook if you look for Nellie's Reader Group, or at www.nelliebrooks.com

I'd love to hear from you. Email me anytime at Nellie@nelliebrooks.com

As always, thank you for reading and reviewing.

I truly appreciate my readers.

Books By This Author

Beach Cove Home

Maisie has avoided Beach Cove for a decade. Now in her early fifties, a desperate search brings her back to her old beach house, new neighbors, and the friends she'd left behind.

Beach Cove Inn

After the tumultuous spring, summer has restored normalcy to the small town of Beach Cove. Ellie's finally ready to grow her store when a letter turns her life upside down.

Beach Cove Secrets

An inhabitant of the small coastal town of Beach Cove hides a terrible secret, but the secret has started to unravel.

Join Sam, Maisie, Ellie and Cate as they uncover the truth and help a growing cast of daughters, friends, and neighbors find love and happiness.

Made in the USA
Monee, IL
16 July 2025